SO-AEW-024

*If Ever
I Return
Again*

CORINNE DEMAS

If Ever
I Return
Again

HARPERCOLLINS*PUBLISHERS*

Please visit the author's website at: www.corinnedemas.com

Library of Congress Cataloging-in-Publication Data
Demas, Corinne.
  If ever I return again / by Corinne Demas.
    p.   cm.
  Summary: In 1856, twelve-year-old Celia Snow sets sail with her parents on her
father's whaling ship and chronicles her subsequent adventures on the more than
two-year voyage in a series of letters written to her cousin Abigail.
  ISBN 0-06-028717-9. — ISBN 0-06-028718-7 (lib. bdg.)
  [1. Whaling—Fiction. 2. Voyages and travel—Fiction. 3. Sea stories.
4. Letters—Fiction.] I. Title.
PZ7.D39145If   2000   99-40586
[Fic]—dc21   CIP
                                                                            AC

Typography by Al Cetta   1 2 3 4 5 6 7 8 9 10   ❖   First Edition

for my daughter, Artemis

Acknowledgements

I am grateful for a Faculty Fellowship from Mount Holyoke College and to the many individuals whose assistance enriched this project, among them: Hope Morrill, Curator of the Cape Cod National Seashore, who provided me with access to the unpublished letters and journal of Bessie Penniman of Eastham; Donald Treworgy, Planetarium Director, Mystic Seaport; Judith M. Downey, Librarian, and Laura Pereira, Library Assistant, Old Dartmouth Historical Society—The New Bedford Whaling Museum; the librarians at the Wellfleet Public Library; the staff of the Wellfleet Historical Society; Peter Carini, Director of Archives, Mount Holyoke College Library; Betsy Cole, Chuck Cole, and Elizabeth L. Will; and for the support of Elaine Lasker vonBruns and Frances Ward Weller; my writing group: Jane Yolen, Ann Turner, Patricia MacLachlan, Anna Kirwan, Leslea Newman, and Barbara Diamond Goldin; my editor, Antonia Markiet; my agent, Tracey Adams; and my family, who were on deck for this whole journey, most especially my husband—my best editor, companion, and compass.

Author's Note

If Ever I Return Again is entirely a work of fiction, yet it had its beginnings in the real-life stories of women who went on whaling cruises. During the middle of the nineteenth century, it was not unusual for the wives of whaling captains to accompany their husbands on journeys, some lasting as long as three to five years. Their children frequently traveled with them, and some were even born on the ship. Many of these women and girls left behind journals that document their remarkable lives at sea. Their adventures, as well as their accounts of the privations and pleasures of daily life on a whaleship, inspired me to write this novel.

My Dearest Abigail—

I could not write for many days. Write! I could not walk nor eat or even talk except to moan and wish that I were home or dead or anywhere but here aboard this ship.

It seemed so smooth at first I thought that I would prove a seaman from the start. How wrong I was! Out past the bay in open ocean the waves were peaked with white, and the ship began to pitch and roll. I felt so sick I stumbled to my cabin where I stayed until this morning, when Papa took me up on deck, saying the air would do me good. Which it has done. Perhaps I have my sea legs, as they call it, at last.

When we left New Bedford it was cold but clear, a fair wind, Papa said. Mother was in her cabin arranging things, but I wanted to be out on deck. I kept my eye on the sweet shoreline till it disappeared from me, bit by bit, till it was just a line. I held it there in memory long after it was gone. Papa passed me his spyglass and through it I could see what had been lost before. Sometime in the world maybe there will be a spyglass so strong I could see not just New Bedford, but all the way back home, to you in Eastham, or even as far as our cousins in Salem, and beyond.

I feel much better now and have begun to eat again, but I am nervous as I had not been when we first started out. The *Jupiter* is sailing smoothly now, but I no longer trust this sea to keep itself this tame, this ship to keep itself this steady. I keep my eye on the modest waves, as if my watching will hold them as they are.

Mr. Prater, the steward, said it was bad luck to set sail on a Friday, but Papa would have none of it—"foolish superstition," he called it, and since the winds were right on the seventeenth, on a Friday we set sail. Of course I know that Papa is right and I take no stock in Mr. Prater's notions, still, it made me uneasy when Mr. Prater shook his head and mumbled, "Let no one say I didn't try to warn you, sir."

Dear Abigail, I am not sure now that I should have said that I would come. Is this what I get for my obstinate ways? Remember how I pleaded with Papa and made such a nuisance of myself until he and Mother agreed that I could join them? I knew if he did not take me now he never would. (A girl is one thing, but once I wear my hair up—to think I ever shall!—he would not have me here with all these men.) I had thought, poor William, so hard for him to be left behind. Though I imagined he would be happier staying there with you with Charles and Sam for company, than here on board with no boy his age. And Papa promised him next trip he'll be the one to go.

And now I think of William in that lovely house on firm ground and envy him. I think of all things firm: the chimney, brick upon brick no wind could tumble, the great stones of the hearth, the trees. These masts were once the tallest, straightest of the trees, but here, deprived of roots and fastened to this ship instead, they are all at the mercy of the whims of the sea. They tilt at the slightest provocation.

There is no land in sight now. Not even a speck of it. No other ships. Nothing here but sea and sky. In all directions it is the same. Nothing to amuse the eye except the shape of clouds. One above that looks like a legless horse, another that looks like the profile of Mr. Soames, the schoolmaster, his nose, though white instead of red.

How desolate this sea! I have never been so far from land before. So far I have to wonder if it really still is there, and did not simply vanish in the sea.

I'm wanted now, below. I'll continue this letter as soon as I am able.

In haste—Celia

continued, next day

Mother is still in her cabin feeling low, so now I have this time all for myself. How luxurious it feels! I am here on deck with my writing box on my lap and my hair knotted up in back in a way that Mother would think undignified, but there is no use trying to write with one's hair blowing about one's face—it's hard enough to keep the paper flat.

Toby is sitting right beside me here. I have been instructed to keep him on his rope, poor thing. The whalemen do not like him underfoot and he has taken to barking at Mr. Grimes, the first mate, who is a sullen sort of man and clearly never fond of dogs. Mother says Toby is not to sleep up on my bunk, but I can't help it if he hops up with me at night when it is dark and I am half asleep, can I? And all those days I was so sick he was my only comfort.

I know once Mother is on her feet again she will have all sorts of tasks to set me to: reading, sewing, improving myself. (Unlike you, my dearest friend, she does not think me quite perfect as I am.) No doubt she sees this as a time when I can be her captive pupil— with no distractions—and an opportunity to fashion me as she would. I think the true reason she at last consented to take me along is that she did not trust me to be left behind. Your mother she adores of course, as any sister would, yet I believe she does not think your mother strong enough to keep me quite in line. You, my dear Abigail, agreeable and gentle as you are, would grow up to be a lady even if you were entirely on your own. But me! Mother has always feared the worst of me. And sometimes dear Abigail—I confess it to you now (I confess everything to you now, this trial at sea makes me want nothing less) sometimes I do small things knowing full well that they will provoke her. At least Papa approves of me, strong-willed as I am. And when Mother gets too difficult I shall appeal to him to pacify her, as he knows how.

How quickly I have covered both sides of this sheet! Mother wanted me to keep a journal on this voyage. She always keeps one, though from what I have seen it is as dull as the ship's logbook where she records our latitude and longitude, the weather and the winds each day. Journals are fine enough, but I much prefer writing to you than writing to myself. For as I write, I imagine you here beside me and feel far less alone. I shall not be able to send this to you until we meet another ship heading back home, but I shall write to you as faithfully as I can—then what a store of letters you shall get from me all at once! And forgive me please if I go on too long and they sometimes sound more like narratives than letters. There is so much time here on a whaler and I have no companion to listen to my tales.

I want nothing more than to get to the Sandwich Islands as quickly as we can and perhaps to get a letter from you there. How shall I stand it being so far from home and you and friends so long?

Adieu for now my dearest Abby. Pray we find a hundred whales as quickly as we can and can soon be speeding back to home to all I hold so dear. Give my love to Grandmother and Grandpa and your parents and Sam and Charles, and please kiss dear Willie for me, if he will let you.

Your most affectionate cousin,
Celia Elizabeth Snow

November 11, 1856

Dearest Abigail,

Here all these days have gone and still I haven't described for you the place that is my home for now and will be for a year or two. (Or, if we have poor luck hunting whales, might be even more. How miserable I'd be!)

The *Jupiter* is so much bigger than Captain Pettengill's schooner. Think of Mr. Moody's barn, afloat, for the *Jupiter* is just about as long, though not, perhaps, as wide across. The ship is divided into three domains. We (Papa, Mother, the mates, and I) inhabit the stern. The seamen's quarters, the forecastle (called fo'c'sle), are in the bow. Steerage is in the middle, home of the cook, steward, cooper, carpenter, and the boat-steerers. They live, then, between us and the common seamen, aptly placed, for their lay (the share of the profits that they will earn at the journey's end) is just between.

The after-cabin is our sitting room, with a sofa, chairs, melodeon, a place for tea, and Papa's desk. There's a window above the sofa, so I can watch the dolphins following us. The forecabin—where we sit at benches round the table (which has been fashioned with a lip along the edges to keep the plates from sliding off, for the *Jupiter* prefers leaning to one side or the other)—has no window, but a skylight to the deck above. It all seems cramped compared with our house on shore, but compared to the fo'c'sle, how luxurious it is! I'm not allowed in the fo'c'sle, but of course I peeked. The bunks are narrow shelves, double-decker, built into the pointed bow, and the men are packed in tight, to sleep and eat and smoke and play cards, and be subjected to each other's company whether they prefer it to solitude or not. Some of the crew have been on many whaling trips, for others, the greenhands, it's the first, some just boys, no older than you. (There is one who gave his name as Richard Piedmont and said he was sixteen, but Mother is sure he is not more than thirteen and has run away from home.)

I am not allowed in steerage either, but I have been there when the cook, Mr. Hodgeson, is not. He snarls if anyone enters the galley, just like Toby guarding a bone. When Mother wants to cook something, she must do all her mixing in our quarters and then the steward has to carry the bowls forward across the rolling deck. Abigail, how you would laugh with me to see chubby Mr. Prater running between our cabin and the galley, trying to keep the contents of the pies (blackberry from our preserves) inside the crust. A touch of salt water is a new ingredient I shall have to learn to like.

The *Jupiter* has three masts, taller than any tree you've ever seen, the front two square-rigged, like a clipper ship, the back rigged fore and aft. (The *Jupiter* is a "bark." A "ship," as you know, has three masts as well, but all its riggings are square.) Each section of sail of course has a name of its own—which I am determined to learn before this trip is over! (don't you love the sound of "mizenmast" and "topgallant" and "flying jib"?)—and there is such a web of ropes you would think that giant spiders had been at work. We have four whaleboats, hung from davits off the rails. I'm not supposed to climb in them, but surely there is no better place to hide out and read. All that is missing is you, my friend, for company. Rebecca, the doll that Grandmother gave me, tries her best, but so far has managed only one expression since we left and has not succeeded in uttering a single word.

Your lonely cousin,

Celia

P.S. Yesterday when I took Rebecca out to get some air, she lost her bonnet in the wind. Papa refused to lower a boat to go in search of it, and says he would not do so if it were Rebecca herself, though I suspect in such a case he might.

November 16, 1856

My Dearest Abigail,

We saw our first whale today! At least the man in the lookout saw it and called out "There blows!" and all the boats were launched in chase. But nothing came of it. I was so excited I could barely breathe and it was sad to see the boats come back with nothing but some very tired men.

When they were all away I let Toby have the run of the deck. There's so much new for him to see and smell, but I'm sure he misses grass and trees, as do we all. Mr. Grimes has informed Mother that he expects the deck to be kept quite clean and Mother passed that information on to me. It seems that Mr. Grimes's shoe had an unfortunate encounter and Toby is to be blamed. I have been outfitted with a scoop.

Mr. Grimes looks like a heron, with a long, beak-like nose and long, skinny legs. He combs his hair back over his bald spot, but in the wind his scalp is well revealed. Mother likes him because she says he is educated and mannerly, but a more dour man I have never met. I've heard he has a wife back at home—he comes from Harwich—but if that is the case I'm sure she's hoping that this voyage is as long as I hope it is short.

The second mate you know, of course, Papa's cousin Isaac Atwood. He is extremely nice but rather dull and hopes to be a captain someday soon. Papa would have made him first mate, I believe, except that Mr. Grimes is so much older and has been a first mate his last few voyages. Mr. Grimes has many grievances and I think Papa was loath to add another one. Mr.

Grimes's chief grievance is that I have been given the cabin that would otherwise have been his, and he was forced to take a lesser one. Papa and Mother have the large cabin on one side of the after-cabin, and I have the smaller cabin on the other side. Small, you would not believe how small, just wide enough to stand beside the bunk, but if you wore a skirt with hoops (though it would be madness of course to wear such a thing on board a ship) you would have to back out as you came in, for there would not be room to turn around. Mr. Grimes has a cabin beside Isaac's and it is not much grander and he feels it, surely. His other grievances include Toby, Mother's plants, which she would have hanging all about, and the melodeon, which takes up room. Animal lover, plant lover, music lover he is not.

Isaac has a sweetheart, Hannah, back at home. He carries her likeness, quite a good one, I believe. He was pleased to show it to me, and I suspect he consults it regularly whether he has someone to show it to or not. Mother likes him well enough, though not as much as Papa does.

The third mate, she likes not at all. And I have saved the best for last, dear Abigail. You see how Mother's taste and mine run counter. His name is Nathaniel Woodbridge, and he would have me call him

Nate, though in Mother's presence Mr. Woodbridge it must be. He's young—too young, Mother says—and though his manners may be wanting, he laughs and jokes and even sings, three things that Mr. Grimes has never done. He has golden curls any girl would envy and fine blue eyes. He is a nephew of Papa's first wife, Demaris (the one who died less than a year after they were married, while Papa was on a voyage), so naturally Mother would be less partial to him than her own kin. Sometimes he winks at me at things that Mother says and once she caught him at it, so she'll think ill of him if ever he gives cause. Papa hopes he turns out all right and settles down a bit, if for no other reason than so that Mother won't find fault.

Mother is quite recovered from her seasickness, and is all about, alas. As I had predicted, she has had me embark upon a course of work that I would gladly trade for the labors of any common seaman on this ship. It's hard enough to sew on level ground, but to keep one's stitches even on a rolling ship is quite another matter. And I've never been so able with a needle, as you know, though Mother says it's not from lack of skill but lack of care. She reads aloud to me from Scripture while I sew, which does not help my sewing or my disposition, and then has me read aloud to her. At least she lets me read what I please when

I am reading on my own, and this stock of books should keep me entertained until we reach the Sandwich Islands.

Two hours every day Mother turns our cabin into a schoolroom and I, her poor, solitary pupil, am subjected to lessons in Latin and in mathematics (we're reviewing decimals now), which she claims I need master if I hope to help Papa, as she has always done, with the navigation.

The sketchbook that you gave me as a farewell gift I shall fill with pleasure. I did a little sketch of Mr. Grimes that Mother said wasn't kind at all, but Papa laughed and Mother scolded him for doing so. "She'll never learn respect if you encourage her this way, Daniel" is what she said.

What a pity it was William who was born the boy and I the girl because I so prefer to be with Papa at the wheel than with Mother with my sewing in my lap. At least I got to raise the flags today. The flags give directions to the whaleboats from the lookout up above, then tell them when to come back to the ship again. They're all in code to keep a secret from other whaleships, though there are none around us now.

We spoke (which means Papa and the other captain converse by voice or flags) a brig, *Jeffery Allyn*, out of New Bedford, yesterday, but the seas were too rough for us to gam and so your letters stay with me.

Good night my dearest Abigail. Pray tomorrow brings us many whales well caught.

Your loving cousin,
Celia

P.S. One of the hogs we brought is due to have piglets any day.

November 27, 1856

My Dearest Abigail,

Thanksgiving Day and here we are in the midst of a grey sea with not a breath of land in sight and our family and friends so far away! I hope that Willie does not miss us too much. Mother worries about him so far away. She's always thought him frailer than he is, no doubt because of the two babies she lost before he was born. (She worried about me, too, I know, when both Willie and I were left at home.) Papa does his best to reassure her that Willie is best off where he is, and when Mother thinks of all the dangers he would be getting into here on board ship, she admits that she is easier knowing he is safe with your family on land. When she stayed at home with Willie and me, instead of accompanying Papa on his cruise, she had spent all her time worrying about Papa. How hard to be a whaling wife, for it seems they must always be missing someone that they love.

I think of you sitting at the table with everyone around you. You cannot imagine how lonely this feels, even with Papa and Mother here, though I should not say that we suffered for wanting anything at our dinner. The cook, Mr. Hodgeson, may be a surly man, and yet he knows his trade, one point, at least, that Mother, Papa, and I all agree upon. Mr. Prater, though somewhat slow, is more agreeable and tries to please (though pleasing Mother is no easy task).

And so we had roast turkey (I gave Toby a piece under the table when Mother wasn't looking, and Nate, I know, fed him a piece as well) and stewed pumpkin and sweet potatoes, biscuits, pies, and preserved peaches, which made me sad again to think of us gathering these peaches from our trees and now it seems so long ago. Isaac, I believe, was very sad, for he misses his Hannah. Mr. Grimes I cannot believe either misses or is missed. Certainly his name should be without its "e." Mother played some hymns on the melodeon, and Papa and Nate sang. Nate has the sweetest tenor voice, but even that will not make Mother fond of him. She finds his laugh too loud, his table manners rough. The men in the fo'c'sle had their feast, too, though not as fine as ours.

Our activities were cut short by the cry "There blows!" and soon the boats were out in pursuit. They harpooned the whale, but then he dove too deep and took a length of line with him and they had to cut him free. So all were disappointed, and it seems unfair to lose a whale as well as all that line. But Papa says when we reach the River LaPlata whaling grounds we shall expect to do well then.

Yesterday morning we spoke another whaler, the *Sea Spray* from Nantucket, out two months before us, a whale ahead. Papa says there was a mutiny on board that ship some three years ago, and this captain, Amos Sloane, and crew are all new. I asked what had happened to the old captain, but Mother would not let him tell me. I shall have to make him tell once we are alone.

The hog has had her piglets, and Papa will let me keep the smallest as my pet. I hope that Toby won't be too jealous. He does not like it when I pet the goats. Annabella is my favorite, though she eats anything she can reach and would even eat this letter if she could.

My love to you on this Thanksgiving, dearest cousin, and I pray that you are all well there as we are here and that we shall quickly fill our casks with oil and next Thanksgiving be home with you again.

Your loving, sea-bound cousin,

Celia

November 29, 1856

Dear Abigail,

We caught our first whale today and you would think I would be filled with joy. Of course I am most truly glad, because we can't return home until our casks are full of oil, and yet . . . The whale's a fearsome creature, but it is a creature nonetheless and thrashes with the lances in its side. And oh, the blood! It spurts, it gushes, it turns the ocean red! I wish there were a way to get the oil but leave the whale unharmed. But I get ahead of myself, for certainly it has been a most exciting day and I am most weary now.

The first cry "There blows!" came right after breakfast. But it was too rough to send the boats out and though by noon it was rough still, it was decided the boats would make a try. All four boats were lowered and set off. Mother would have me remain in the cabin, where we'd been employed in the great adventure of mending sheets, until the work was done, but I did not want to miss a moment of the chase. She'll

· 17 ·

tell Papa that I disobeyed, but surely I was already outside on deck and could not hear her calling me.

There were three sperm whales but they were moving fast and though the boats gave chase they could not get close enough to strike. And then another whale was seen and this time the waistboat reached it and the boatsteerer threw his harpoon and it caught fast. Then what a ride they had! I could not blame the whale for trying to escape and yet I feared so for the boat, which was so small the whale could flip it with its tail. At last the whale was tired out and they threw the lance in its side. Finally it was killed and they towed it back. And now it is tied up here beside the ship, and it is so large it looks as if it is another vessel lying beside us. And so I saw my first sperm whale up close. The blackfish that we have seen washed up upon the beach at home are like herrings to this whale—it would take a dozen or more of them to equal its weight.

This whale is half as long as our ship, with a head the size of your bedroom, a long jaw with teeth the size of my hand, and an eye that's tiny for the whale but big as a dinner plate. A sad eye, and dead. To think I have seen the biggest creature there exists on earth! And it seems strange, doesn't it, that such a giant could be felled by little men in little boats.

They've commenced cutting into the whale. They take the blubber off, then cut it into squares and mince it up. Then they shall begin boiling.

I have named my piglet Ophelia. Nate brought her up to me, all swaddled in a canvas. You should have seen the look on Mr. Grimes's face!

I shall add more to this letter tomorrow.

next day

Mother spoke to Papa about my behavior yesterday and to pacify her he was stern with me and told me my first duty was to obey my mother.

"But surely, Papa," I said, "you would not want me to miss out on the most exciting thing that's happened all these weeks. The mending would obviously wait, though the whale would not."

"There will be other whales," he said.

"But not other first whales," said I, and of course Papa had to laugh and even Mother smiled, although I could tell she did her best to keep her lips quite straight.

I can't think what I would do without Papa! Can you imagine just me and Mother cooped up here on this ship alone? I would surely have to mutiny!

I asked Papa about the *Sea Spray*, and he would

only say that there had been trouble aboard the ship between the officers and the men and the captain had left his post.

And so I asked Isaac, and he, not knowing that Mother wanted the story kept from me, blurted out, "That terrible business! The captain was murdered by his own crew!" It made my blood run cold to think of that. Of course Papa is a fair and kind master, well liked by all his crew. The *Sea Spray*'s captain must have been a cruel man to inspire such a death. But maybe not. Perhaps he was a fine captain and his crew a band of murderers. I must ask Isaac more when Mother is not around. I have looked over our crew and they don't appear the least like murderers, except for the cook, the blacksmith (who has a nose that was flattened in a fight), and two dark-skinned seamen who go by English names, John Davis and William Greene, but are from the Cape Verde Islands and speak to each other in a language I am told is Portuguese.

We now have a tryworks going on our ship, the great brick furnace all fired up. The blubber is boiled until it's reduced to oil. I've never imagined such a sickening smell. There is nowhere on this ship that you can go to escape it. It's not a smell that just assaults your nose, but a smell so thick you could clench it in your fist. I've tried breathing only through my mouth, but even so, the smell clogs my throat and makes me gag and turns my stomach inside out. Mother says she learned to get used to it, but I wonder if I ever shall. Everything is smoky and the decks are awash in grease. I've had to keep Toby in the cabin, where he barks and howls. It makes Mr. Grimes clench his teeth, which makes me smile. Nate says I need keep my eye on Mr. Grimes lest he chuck Toby overboard when I'm not looking, but I'm sure he's only teasing me.

Mother caught Nate swearing and had Papa speak to him. I far prefer Nate's swearing to Mr. Grimes's scowls, but Mother approves of Mr. Grimes no matter how he glowers. "He's a gentleman," she reminds me, as if that is enough!

Mother likes Isaac well enough, but Mr. Grimes is quick to point out any faults to Mother because he sees Isaac as a threat to his position, and Mother always believes what Mr. Grimes says. He is not one to lie outright, but has a clever way of fashioning the truth so he comes out the best.

We spoke another whaler today, the *Devonshire* out of Falmouth. Tomorrow maybe we can have a gam. If they are headed home I will give them my packet of letters for you.

Your loving, tired cousin,
Celia

December 1, 1856

My Dearest Abigail,

So much news! This morning we had our first accident on board. The decks are covered with slippery oil and Mother fell and sprained her ankle. It's swollen and sore, though not broken, for which we're very thankful. The benefit is that now she can't follow me about and tell me what I mustn't do, and so I'll have some freedom for several days at least. The problem is that she expects me to wait on her and is feeling very sorry for herself (although I think she also enjoys this spell as invalid). It's certainly easier to be solicitous towards someone when they suffer but don't complain at all, than when they complain too much. I know you think me most unkind! Papa's had them wash the deck, but with the boiling going on it is impossible to keep it clean. Papa is concerned about my slipping, too, but I am not so clumsy, though I admit I often run when I am told to walk.

In the late afternoon we gammed with the *Devonshire*. Papa wanted me to stay with Mother, but I pleaded so, he finally gave in when Isaac (who knew how much I wanted to go) said he would see to all of Mother's wants. We could not put it off till tomorrow because the *Devonshire* is homeward bound and eager to be off. I took over with me the latest newspapers and all our letters (Mother quickly wrote her own) and a jar of plum preserves.

The captain of the *Devonshire*, Joseph Strickley, was very cordial. He's been away from home for three years, and has a wife and four children, the youngest who was born after he left and he has never seen. I wished his wife and children had been aboard for it's been so long since I saw a person my own age. The *Devonshire* has 2,476 barrels of oil, which is not as good as Mr. Strickley hoped. He says the whales don't seem so plentiful now as they once were, and he caught only two right whales in all. He was most grateful for the papers, the most recent he has seen in a long time. He gave me several oranges to take back and three chickens, which was most generous. The chickens, I think, were meant for eating, but one has such pretty speckled feathers I won't have her for our table, but as a pet. Papa says we'll have a genuine ark if this keeps up.

Captain Strickley says he met a whaler once that had a pony and a cart aboard, but I'm not sure if he was teasing. Can you see me, Abigail, driving around the deck with a pony and a cart? That would surely put a frown on Mr. Grimes's face!

The oranges put Mother in a happy mood on our return and she thought it most generous of Captain

Strickley to give us so many, and three hens. I asked Nate what to name the chicken and he suggested Moses.

"It's a girl," I said, and he asked me if I was sure, and for a moment made me think, and then we both laughed. So I have named her Miriam, the name of Moses' sister.

Mother had me read the story of Miriam in the Bible. The Lord got angry at Miriam when she spoke out against Moses and punished her with leprosy (which I think unnecessarily cruel of him). Then Moses pleaded with the Lord to cure Miriam, and so he did. A lot of the stories in the Bible don't make sense to me, and that is one of them.

The chicken doesn't seem to mind her name and cocks her head in a way that makes you think she's listening closely to what you say. Toby barked at her and she got in such a flurry she nearly turned the cabin upside down and so I have to keep them apart or Mother will change her mind and we'll have Miriam for dinner.

Our whale gave us 116 barrels of oil. Papa hopes to get at least 2,500, as much as Captain Strickley. That means we need to get twenty-one whales at least (if my calculations are correct) before we can go home. And so far we've had only one! I've never thought of it quite this way before. Oh, Abigail, how long this voyage seems now, how long it stretches ahead of me! A few weeks aboard a whaleship—why, that seems tolerable enough—but years? As I'm twelve now, that means if we are out three years I will be fifteen when I next am home. And you, dear Abigail, will be nearly seventeen. Shall we know each other? And Willie, my sweet little brother, will be eleven—old enough to be a cabin boy. It's true I knew all this before I chose to come. But while we may know about things ahead of time, it's not until we're <u>in</u> them that we know what they are really like.

I miss everything of home. If only I had stayed with you—what fun we could have had together! I'd miss Papa sorely, and yes, even Mother, too (though she so often vexes me), but that would be nothing to all that I am missing now.

Pray that we come across a school of whales and fill our barrels before this season is up.

Dear Abigail, please give Willie a big hug for me, whether he likes it or not. I can't wait until we reach the Sandwich Islands so I can get my mail (I trust there will be a letter for me there from you) and I can read your words and imagine that I hear your voice.

Your gamming cousin,
Celia

December 2, 1856

My Dearest Abigail,

Papa is beginning to instruct me, whenever there's a chance, in all things navigational: how to read a compass, read a chart, and read the sky for what's to come. I would learn all I can. Mother has always helped him take his sights, and chart the course, and I would like to do that, too.

Today Papa used one of Captain Strickley's oranges for my lesson in latitude and longitude. The top and bottom were the earth's poles, and with his penknife Papa cut a circle around the middle for the equator, then more circles for other parallels. When he peeled the orange, the sections were the meridians, running from one pole to the other.

Then we ate the whole lesson up.

I wonder how they ever came up with such an idea as longitude and latitude, all those imaginary lines— the parallels and meridians—dividing up the entire globe. On land you could actually mark them in the ground. Here at sea they will always be invisible, but it's comforting to know that they are there. It means that every square of ocean is identified, with a location for a name (right now we are at Latitude 20° 12' N, Longitude 42° 22' W), so you are always someplace, even if you don't know it at the time.

Papa's sextant is a tricky thing to use. You have to line up the two mirrors exactly right, then catch the reflection of the sun through the scope and move it so it just perches on the horizon. All this with the ship bouncing up and down! We shoot the sun (that's what it's called) if the sky is clear, morning, noon, and afternoon, and at twilight we shoot the moon, the planets, and that lovely, faithful star Polaris. We use our readings to calculate our angles of latitude and longitude, with the help of Bowditch's *Practical Navigator*, our Nautical Almanac, and our chronometer (which is set at Greenwich Mean Time). I am afraid I must admit that all the geometry that Mother has been making me learn has proved most necessary. Trigonometry is next, but not tonight! Tonight I shall be dreaming about oranges.

Your navigating cousin,
Celia

December 7, 1856

My dear, dear Abigail,

I haven't been able to write for several days. I am barely alive to write at all. I've never been so close to death! I know, dear Abigail, that you must think that I exaggerate—but how I wish that that were true. Words on paper are too mild to convey what this storm was like, to tell you what I survived. We are still recovering, and it will be days more before we have dried out.

You would not believe it to see the ocean now, lying docilely, with orderly, low waves, nor to see the sky, blue with little white puffs of clouds. All innocent the two of them, as if they hadn't turned so fierce, and changed till they were unrecognizable. It's strange, isn't it, that no matter how rough the waves, no matter how the wind tears up the water, afterwards it can lie as flat as if it never was touched; no scars are left. The sky can be filled with lightening and black clouds, and then later be sweetly blue, with no trace of anything at all.

We were having dinner when it started up. The sky got oddly dark and the wind came up so fast the ship toppled on its side. All went wild: dishes, food, forks, and bottles. I would have thought it amusing to watch the potatoes roll right off the plates, the fish to fly across the cabin, but Papa leaped up from his seat as did Mr. Grimes and Isaac and Nate and all ran on deck and I knew that something fearful was happening. The ship righted herself for a short while and I got my breath, but then we were hit again.

If the table had not been nailed to the cabin floor it would have gone flying, too. As it was, everything not attached went crashing all about, including me and the melodeon. I have bruises on my arm from being smashed against the wall. The melodeon suffered somewhat worse, and Mother hopes the ship's carpenter will be able to repair it.

Mr. Prater looked very white. "I shall ask the cook to make a second dinner," he said. But there was no need for that for there was no way that any of us could eat.

Until you've been in a storm at sea you can't imagine how it is. Standing on the beach in a nor'easter, you can feel the wind and the rain, but no matter how it roars, no matter how high the waves, how hard they crash, you have solid ground beneath your feet. The ship is like a piece of driftwood in the waves, tossed up high and dropped down again. Nothing is solid, nothing is level, nothing is sure.

The waves were higher than the rooftops, high as the spire of the church. We climbed up to the very crests, then dropped down into the troughs between them. The waves were like walls on either side of us and I thought they would close right over our heads and we would be swallowed up. The sea crashed across the decks and though the doors and windows and hatches were closed tight, everything was soaked. This went on all night and into the next morning, too, and I thought that it would never end. I did not sleep one wink, nor did anyone aboard this ship, even Toby, who trembled in my arms.

Papa came to comfort me and assure me that all would soon be well, but he was not able to keep us company for long. Mother, to my great surprise, was hardy through it all. "I've seen many storms," she said. And it made me wonder how if she had lived through a storm like this one she could ever want to go out on a ship again. I'm certain that I never shall! She was most amazing through it all. She did not succumb to terror as I would have thought she would, but consulted with Papa what was to be done and then went to work fastening things down and cleaning up and seeing to what she could. (Her ankle is recovered now.) She was so kind to me and took me in her arms as if I were a baby still and sang to me old songs.

"Will we all die?" I asked her then.

"Oh, no, we'll be all right. I have absolute faith in your father and this ship. And I have faith in God."

I thought of that. The strange thing is I have more faith in Papa than in God—I dare to tell you this! For God, I know, has let ships sink, and many seamen have been lost at sea, and captains and their families, too. And certainly those other daughters prayed to God and were not saved! But Papa, I know, can get through any storm, and the *Jupiter* is a ship he trusts, and so

I trust it too. And that was where my comfort lay.

But oh, dear Abigail, what an easy life I had until this time. I had no idea what fear was. I said I was afraid of any number of things, but if you are on dry land there is nothing that is truly frightening, nothing like the sea.

I must close now. We have all the bedding out on the deck and are hoping the sunshine will last. My china hair jar, the one that Grandmother gave me, is in shards. (How foolish I was to leave it on my nightstand!)

With love to all of you, my dearest family. To think Willie may have been an orphan! And if we never make it home and he becomes one, I know that you will love him for me as if he is your brother, too.

Kiss him a hundred times, dear Abigail, and think of me, your poor cousin, Celia, and pray that we never have another storm like this.

Your Celia

December 10, 1856

My Dearest Abigail,

Mother is back to her most irritating self and I have been confined to quarters, which is most unfair. The men are still celebrating crossing the line. (One dressed up as King Neptune, and all the greenhands were shaved and doused with a pail of water. Then they were pronounced "old salts." Papa permitted everyone a glass of grog.) And I can't be on deck!

Now you know my punishment, so let me detail what Mother perceives to be the crime and you be judge.

We were just crossing the equator and Nate came up to me with his spyglass and bade me have a look. And there, through the glass, I saw a faint line. Now I am not so foolish as to imagine that the equator is something you can see, like a line drawn on the very water itself, so I guessed that Nate was tricking me, and sure enough, he had laid a hair across the glass. I called foul and pretended I would strike him with the spyglass except he ducked and dashed away, with me in pursuit. Finally I had him trapped against the whaleboat and I lifted the spyglass high, laughing so hard I could barely hold it still, and Mother came up sternly and sent me down below. She says it is unseemly for the captain's daughter to be chasing after mates on deck and I am too old for such nonsense.

But I wonder if perhaps it is a case of me being too young rather than too old. For in truth while I was there with Nate face to face, so close, he looked at me in such a way I thought—oh, Abigail, dare I tell you what I thought? (This is why I write in letters to you rather than a journal, for Mother might read my journal but in letters I can be private if I chose.) I thought what it would be like to have him kiss me. There, I've said it now. I can picture your sweet face as you read these lines. I shock you I am sure. But you have not seen Nate and if you did, I think it would be less shocking.

For your sake, though, I will claim I mean the kind of kiss he would bestow upon his sisters. He has three younger sisters, he's told me, back at home, and I can imagine he is quite the favorite of them. I envy them having him as their brother. (Not that I would trade in dear Willie, but a little brother is quite another thing.) Of course Nate's sisters are so far away and see him so little, whereas I get to see him every day.

But I have had my little revenge against Mother for this imprisonment. When Isaac came down into the forecabin (Mother was still with her sewing up on deck) I decided to find out more about that mutiny on the *Sea Spray*. I thought Isaac might think it imprudent to tell me about the captain's fate, so I said, "I heard they tied him up with ropes and weighed him down with stones and threw him overboard."

"Oh, no," said he, "they slew him, with a harpoon in his heart."

That took my breath for a moment, you can be sure. And I could tell that Isaac, once again, was sorry he had told me, though he did not see that I had trapped him into doing so.

"What a beastly man he must have been to deserve such a fate at the hands of his crew," I said.

"Oh, no," insisted Nate. "He had a reputation for being a decent and gentle man. It was his crew that were the beasts."

"His mates as well?" I asked.

"The second mate was the treacherous one, the one who plotted the mutiny. He was later brought to trial and hanged. The first mate was faithful, and when he went to the captain's aid was slain himself by a blow to his head."

"And the third mate?" I asked, thinking of Nate.

"No third mate on that ship. The cabin boy hid out and saw it all."

"I guess that Papa would do well then to keep his eye on you, Isaac," I said, smiling.

Then poor Isaac got very red. And I said, quickly, "I'm sure in our case it's Mr. Grimes we better watch out for. For you, Isaac, I know we can trust with everything."

"I'm quite sure, Celia, that your father is in no danger, nor ever will be. This is a decent crew, and Mr. Grimes an honorable man."

Poor Isaac! He is kind and dear and gullible. He will make his Hannah a fine and gentle husband. But for myself I think I would prefer a husband with a bit more vinegar. And then there is the unavoidable fact that Isaac is not a handsome man. I do not mean that he is ugly—no, his countenance is pleasant, his person most agreeable, his teeth as straight and white as you could hope. It's just that his chin is abbreviated, his nose is undistinguished, his eyes a bit too close together, and his hair so thin and flat. It's not his fault for sure, because he is so nice he deserves to be the handsomest of men. And indeed I'm sure his Hannah finds him so.

Mother came down to fetch some thread (and no doubt to check on me), and asked what Isaac and I were talking about. I said, "The Sandwich Islands." Isaac looked a bit startled by this—he is a man uncomfortable with untruths of any sort. Mother went back up on deck well contented. I've told you that she does not like Isaac as much as she likes Mr. Grimes, yet she thinks him a suitable companion for her daughter. He is kin, after all, though not as educated as Mr. Grimes (although I suspect Mr. Grimes is not as learned as he makes out to be).

Of course, dear Abigail, as you would guess, it's Nate whom I would most have as my companion.

Your cousin Celia,

Old Salt

December 17, 1856

My Dearest Abigail,

We got a right whale at the beginning of this week, and he brought us more oil than twice the whale we caught before. So I will count that as three whales towards our twenty-one. Yet what a small quantity we have to show for all these days and weeks at sea!

Mother stayed below for two days while the try-works were going until the decks were cleared again, fearing for her footing. She would have me stay safely below as well, but fortunately Toby needs to be let out, and he can't run free when the boiling is going on, so I must keep him on a rope. And that dog needs lots of air or he won't thrive. And I need to be on deck to do my navigation. Papa has me take my sights, then check my readings against his. Now that we are south of the equator we can no longer see Polaris, our trusty Pole star, and so we must manage as best we can with all the others.

I love to watch the boiling at night. It's like a party up on deck, the fire all great against the dark sky. In the distance there was another whaleship that must have had good luck as well, for they were boiling, too. And that was wonderful to see their light at night across the sea. Why, it looked almost like a bonfire on shore, a bit of land. And the sea didn't seem so empty and us so small and alone with at least another ship there. Perhaps we will gam with them tomorrow.

I sat with Papa, and Toby curled up at our feet. We could have been us at home before the fire in our hearth. The crew was singing songs and their voices sounded so lovely echoing against the water. We don't have a shanty man aboard this ship, but our boatsteerer Joseph Sylva (he is a Portuguese, but his English is as good as mine) has a velvety, rich voice that goes as low as the depth of the sea, and the notes rumble and hang in the air. Papa and I joined in with the singing (though if Mother were up on deck with us I am not sure that she would approve).

My favorite song is "It Was Pleasant and Delightful," and although I've heard it now so many times, I always cry at the end when the seaman says farewell to his true love, and we sing along with the last line, "And if ever I return again, I will make you my bride." Papa hugged me close to him and I thought how lonely it must have been for him the years he was at sea alone. I never want Papa to be alone, away from all of us. And even if I hate the sea and its storms and all that they can bring, surely it is better to be with Papa than to be at home imagining him a solitary man on the deck looking across the dark ocean to the place where home would be, if only he could see it.

Oh, Abigail, you don't know how lucky you are to have both: your dear father with you and your home on land. What most girls our age take for granted, and which can never be mine. For either I have home on land and Papa far away, or else I have his company and must give up everything else I love.

Your shanty-singer cousin,
Celia

Christmas, 1856

Dearest Abigail,

My first Christmas away from home, away from all of you, away from Winter—why, away from Christmas itself, it seems. Everything is so un-Christmas-like here. It's hot, hot as summer. So hot the seamen go around without shirts upon their backs and yesterday some of them went swimming beside the ship. Mother would have me miss out on watching all the fun (they swim without any clothing on!), but luck was with me and she fell asleep in her chair (she's taken to napping so much these days) and I took full advantage to watch. (I kept to the stern of the boat, but leaned over the rails.)

What a lark they had! I wish I were a seaman! There, did I shock you? I'll shock you even more and say I wish I could toss off all these clothes and plunge into that cool water! And I can swim, remember?— for the summer I was eight, when Papa was home he taught me how. (He says he would not take me or Mother aboard his ship unless we could.) You'd be surprised how many seamen don't know how to swim. I've heard it said they think that if the ship were wrecked you would have a quick and easy death if you didn't know how to swim, but would struggle and suffer longer if you did. A foolish notion, Papa says. More than likely, if you were shipwrecked in cold water you'd die of the cold before you had a chance to drown, and if the water was warm the sharks would get you first.

Neither Mr. Grimes nor Isaac swam, but Nate joined in and he and Jonathan Eldridge (he was a student at Yale but took off some time to see the world— Mother suspects his family does not yet know) both did lovely dives from the whaleboat (they'd lowered one for the occasion) and one of the Portuguese, William Greene, dove right off the ship itself! They all had to give up the sport when the sharks came around. They killed a shark and brought it up on deck. It is as fearsome a creature as you can imagine. We'll have shark meat for dinner, but not for Christmas dinner, I am thankful for that!

Mother told me to hang up my stocking and so I did (we have no fireplace, of course, so I hooked it on the woodstove in our cabin) and in the morning it was full so I guess that Santa Claus can navigate on sea as well as travel by land. (I spotted Papa by the stocking, but I did not let him know. He and Mama would be disappointed, I think, if they knew I no longer believed in Santa Claus, especially since without Willie with us I am the only child around.) I got a little tin of peppermints, some walnuts, silk ribbon, a string of glass beads, and a gold coin! And Mama made a beautiful outfit for Rebecca—a red velvet dress with a matching cape lined with silk and a hat with a plume. Too elegant for a whaleship, no doubt, but someone aboard must be in fashion! And Rebecca never has to get her skirts messy dragging along a deck. I shall need to keep her below if there are heavy winds, for this is one bonnet I would hate to donate to the sea!

How dear of Mother to have been working on this for me—for she must have been doing it in secret at night while I was sleeping, and must have been so careful to hide it all away. This is what is so perplexing about Mother. She is thoroughly irritating most of the time and then she does kind things that make me feel ashamed of myself for disliking her. If she can't be kind all of the time I wish she would be more consistently awful so I could dislike her to my heart's content without reproach.

I gave Papa some handkerchiefs I had embroidered with his initials. He was sweet and acted as if he were truly surprised, although he could see me working on them for days. For Mother I painted a little scene of our house, and Papa had the carpenter make a frame for it. It is such a fine frame any picture would be greatly improved by it. If tears of happiness be a measure of success then this gift was that, though of course Mother was crying as well for the memory of home and all we left behind, especially dear Willie.

I would have liked nothing better than to have gotten a Christmas present from Nate, but all I got was a cheerful Christmas greeting. It is not rational for me to have hoped for a gift, but disappointment is not a rational creature.

Later

For Christmas dinner we had quite a feast: pork roast and potatoes and pudding and pie, but in truth it was the kind of meal that required a snowstorm outside. Even you, my generous cousin, would be hard pressed to appreciate all that steaming food when it was so hot you had sweat collecting in the unmentionable parts of your body and dripping off your brow.

Toby got a great bone for his Christmas treat and was deliriously happy. That's what's so appealing about dogs—they can be made truly happy with so little, whereas we humans require such a lot. All the animals got extra rations and my piglet, Ophelia, got an apple. (I did not inform her that one of her brothers graced our table.) The men in the fo'c'sle arranged a concert of carols and we all attended, sitting out on deck, even Toby, who wore a red ribbon for the occasion, and my hen, Miriam, who added a few notes of her own.

I try not to think about Christmas at home. When I do, I picture coming down the stairs and turning into the parlor and seeing the Christmas tree all twinkling with candles. I think about the way Christmas at home smells—pine boughs and bayberry and baking. (Everything on this ship smells of whale oil—there is no escaping it.) I think of all the family around—but I hold myself right there. For I remember those Christmases when Papa was at sea and we did not even have a letter from him and did not know where he was and how he was but knew only that he was missing all of us. And so that is my consolation. I would rather be here on this ship with Papa than home for Christmas without him.

And so I wish you the happiest of Christmases my dear Abigail. I can think of no other present I want from you than a letter.

Merry Christmas to you all, and all my love,
Celia

December 27, 1856

My Dearest Abigail,

The clouds have been so thick for days we have not seen the sun or moon or stars. Our sextant is of no use at all. Papa has been teaching me dead reckoning, which is the only way to navigate when you are cheated of the sky. It has nothing to do with graveyards, I assure you. Papa says "dead" came from "deduced," which means you have to figure out where you are based on where you were before. All you need to know is your course (the compass tells you that) and the distance you have traveled. Papa heaves out the chip log (a piece of wood at the end of a line with knots tied evenly along it) and cries out, "Turn!" Then I turn the sand-glass over and cry out, "Done!" The second the half-minute is run out, I cry out, "Stop!" and Papa stops the reel. We count how many knots ran out and know how fast we're sailing, and then Papa has me do my calculations to learn how far we've gone.

I thought I had it all figured out until Papa reminded me about the current.

"You mean we could have a speed of ten knots and yet not be traveling any distance at all?"

"You always have to account for drift, Celia," said Papa. Then he saw my face. "Don't worry, Sweetheart," he said. "It takes some time to learn all this. And you have a real instinct for it."

"Oh, Papa," I said, "I wish we were whaling in Great Pond!"

Papa laughed. "I'm not sure bass and pickerel are very good for trying out."

On Saturday we were passed by a clipper ship— she showed her longitude, chalked on a blackboard (Papa was glad to see our chronometer is right), as she flew by, all sleek and proud. I wondered if she was carrying a letter from you to me. Mother says envy is not an admirable trait, but even she could not help but join me in envying that ship's speed. Papa tells me the men on clipper ships refer to us whalers as "old tubs" (Nate said that's not the worst they call us, but Mother gave him a look that made him say no more), but Papa believes a whaler is the perfectly built ship, because it goes fast enough yet can carry a thousand barrels of oil in her hull, provisions for thirty men for many months, and weather any seas and any storms and even Arctic ice. Clipper ships are all speed and show and Papa wouldn't choose to be on one and so neither would I.

Your very-much-alive reckoning cousin,
Celia

P.S. The glass is going down. Papa says a storm is brewing.

January 11, 1857

My dear, dear Abigail,

We've made it around the Horn! And I am still alive. I never want to round the Horn again in my whole life except that is the way we shall be coming back. So if I want to ever see home again, and Willie, and you, I have no choice. But I won't talk of it, and I won't think about it. I won't write to you about what it is like to lie on a wretched bunk so sick you don't care if the ship sinks or not, the ship rolling and pitching as if gravity no longer existed and shaking blow after blow, struggling to keep afloat, the sea crashing over the decks and the masts straining so I feared they would snap off. Days of this! And then a break. And then days more! I could not sleep. I could not eat. I could barely drink and when I did I could not hold it down for long.

Isaac was very sweet and congratulated me, for now, he says, I am an experienced seaman. Mr. Grimes was injudicious enough to remark at dinner that that was one of his better trips around the Horn and said in his most matter-of-fact way that it was usual to lose a man or two if not a total ship. Even Mother, who usually approves of anything that loathsome man has to say, ahemmed and changed the subject before he could go on any longer. It's incomprehensible to me why she tolerates that man at all, let alone claims to admire him!

Our reward for surviving the trip around the Horn was a small, deliciously green island, uninhabited except for marvelous fruit. I went to shore in one of the whaleboats and here's the curious thing: my body, all used to walking on a rolling ship, forgot how to walk on firm land and at first I staggered and swayed.

"I told you it would take a while to get your land legs back," Papa said.

The seamen gorged themselves on fruit—peaches, figs, and grapes (I did so myself), and Mother had them bring back bushels full. What a fine navigator Papa is to find this island in the first place. It is quite surrounded by sea and you could so easily miss it altogether. I suppose there are many tiny islands like this, spread all across this part of the sea as goodies for exhausted seamen who made it round the Horn.

Toby went wild on the island, running up and down the beach like a crazy dog. I took off my shoes and stockings and ran with him. I trailed my fingers in the sand and wrote my name in great curling letters. Mother didn't want Toby in the whaleboat with us going back (I could hardly blame her since he kept shaking and spraying us with sandy water), but there was no other way to get him to the ship. When we got back on board he was so tired from his frolic he collapsed on deck. I think I shall not have him sleep in my bunk tonight!

I had a moment to talk with Nate yesterday. Mother had fallen asleep on the sofa (it seems as if she's often tired now), so I could do as I pleased, and I went up on deck. There was Nate, and it wasn't his watch, and I found myself asking him, quite by chance, if he knew anything about Papa's first wife, his aunt. I guess it was a question I had always wanted to ask but never had the opportunity to do so before. I knew her name—Demaris—for it is on her headstone, which is in our family plot, and I knew she was only twenty-three when she died.

Nate told me he had grown up hearing all about her. He called her "Merry," for that was her nickname—isn't that a lovely name?

"Do you know if she was beautiful?" I asked him.

"Oh, yes, very beautiful," he said.

I picture her with golden curls (Nate's hair, grown long), a sweet singing voice like his, and an angelic countenance.

"What did she die of?" I asked.

"They said it was consumption," he said.

"But it wasn't?"

"I believe she died of love," he said. And at that very moment the loathsome Mr. Grimes appeared (he has a way of appearing out of nowhere, I feel as if he is always lurking in the shadows, spying on me), and so we both turned to the rail and pretended we were just studying the sea, for I can imagine Mr. Grimes reporting to Mother that Nate and I were up to something on the deck and he thought that she should know. It is none of Mr. Grimes's business what Nate and I talk about it.

Can you imagine being cut off in the midst of something quite remarkable as that? I had no more opportunity of talking with Nate alone and have been wild to find out more. Demaris was married to Papa then, so what does that mean—that she died of love? I shall have to find some way to talk with Nate alone again very soon.

We had a rainstorm this morning and collected lots of fresh water for the washing. It's funny how the men on board a whaler do all kinds of women's work they would not do at home. Not only do they wash but they sew as well, and some of them are as fine with a needle and thread as Mother. Everyone does his own laundry except Mr. Grimes and a young seaman named Silas Hathaway who has joined the ship to improve his eyesight and comes from a wealthy family (as he has let everyone know), who pay another seaman to do theirs for them. Now clothes lines are strung all around the deck. Mother has hung our underclothing to dry beneath the sheets, for it would not do to have the men admiring them.

Good night, Dear Abigail. I shall write again as soon as I find out the rest of Nate's story.

Your curious cousin,
Celia

P.S. My piglet, Ophelia, is getting larger every day. Isaac warned me that the cook has his eye on her. What shall I do when she gets really big?

January 17, 1857

My Dear Abigail,

We got another whale which made a hundred and ten barrels, and managed to pick up the carcass of a dead whale, which, though it brought only twenty barrels, was quite the easiest sort of whale to catch. Would they all just died or were killed somehow and we could just sail around and gather them up like seaweed. So we're two whales closer to coming home! (Or, to be more accurate, a whale and a half.)

I know you care much less about the tallies of whale oil than the news I have to tell—but I could not resist teasing you a little. I finally got my chance to talk with Nate again, and I think you will agree with me that the tale was worth the wait.

Nate told me Papa and Demaris were married only a few months when he shipped out as mate on a whaler. He'd been gone close to a year when she got word that his ship had wrecked and all men lost. It was wintertime. She got ill and said she had no will to live.

"But Papa wasn't in a wreck," I said. "He wasn't lost at sea!"

"Your father had left that ship in the Sandwich Islands," said Nate. "The captain was incompetent and given to heavy drinking and your father wouldn't sail with him any longer. He reported the captain's behavior to the Consulate and got passage back on another whaler. But the captain was never brought to trial, the sea passed judgement on him first—unfortunately taking the whole crew along."

"And Merry?"

"The news of the shipwreck was brought to her before your father was able to return. When he got home she had already died."

When I heard this I just stood there, Abigail. I could not say another word. Imagine, she died not knowing he was alive!

"And that," said Nate, "would account for why your mother doesn't want to be left at home. She'd rather suffer the miseries of life at sea than suffer the worries of being left back home. And I for one can hardly blame her."

"Why did no one tell me?"

"It's an awkward situation, as you can see. Your

mother owes all her present happiness—her husband, children—to my aunt's death. I imagine it was decided that this bit of family history remain untold, and so I would be obliged if you kept it so. Can I count on your discretion?"

"Of course, Nate!" I cried. "You have my solemn word." (I'm sure he would not think I betray this confidence by writing thus to you, for you, I am certain, will be discreet as well.)

And so now I know the tragedy of Demaris. It's just like Shakespeare's *Romeo and Juliet*. (Except in this case Romeo survives.) Can you imagine how my poor Papa must have felt to return home after all those months of longing only to find his bride dead! If Demaris had not gotten that false report, she would not have died, and Papa wouldn't have married my mother and I wouldn't have been born, nor Willie, either. Now I see why Mother dislikes Nate so. Every time she looks at him she is reminded of Papa's first bride, his first love!

If I marry a whaling captain I believe I shall accompany him on all his voyages, in spite of all the miseries and terrors of the sea, for anything is better than to be waiting for news. But here's the predicament, it's far more likely I would marry someone younger (can you guess who I would hope that someone to be?) who is not a captain yet, only a mate, and mates can't bring their wives along. There's Isaac's poor Hannah, waiting for him. Isaac ate the "home cake" that Hannah gave him when he left to celebrate going around the Horn. Hannah had put so much liquor in it, it nearly exploded when he opened the tin. He shared it with us all and it was quite a treat. Mother would let me have only one piece and that a small one, too!

Good-bye for now, my dear cousin. Whatever news you hear of us, do not give up on us ever, just in case it is false news. I would hate to have you mourn for us unless it was absolutely necessary.

Your cousin,
Celia

January 23, 1857

My Dear Abigail,

We gammed this week with the *Ranger* out of Edgartown, Captain Winslow and his family. They have two children, a boy named Reuben, whom they call Robin, who is nine, and a girl named Content, who is just eight. They are both as brown as whalemen and run quite wild on the ship, climb the riggings and scamper about like monkeys. Their mother is a mild, impractical sort of woman who lets them look out for themselves. Their father is quite obese and good-humored and thinks everything the children do amusing. Neither parent seems the least concerned about the dangers they may encounter. Both children were born upon the ship and seem as agile as seamen. They've survived innumerable perils, including a storm so strong the ship was dismasted!

I wish I could have Content's freedom, and shouldn't mind a bit racing about barefoot with my hair in tangles. She has exactly the same privileges as her brother. Indeed the two look so much alike, and she wears clothing like her brother's, that you would not know for sure which was the boy, which one the girl. I asked Mother if she would make me a pair of denim trousers like Content's, but she was not enthusiastic about the idea. (We wear our skirts so much shorter here, above our ankles—you can't have them trailing on wet decks—but trousers would be so much more convenient!)

We brought them some eggs, a pie, and a jar of preserves, and they were so generous as to bestow upon us a basket of pineapples, several books, and a turkey (ugly thing!).

Mother would have liked, I could tell, to take the entire family in hand, but restrained herself from doing so. Mary Winslow is such a sweet and charming woman, even if she seems a little befuddled, that even

Mother didn't have the heart to set her right.

Yesterday they all came to our ship. Content and Robin were thrilled by Toby. He performed all three of his tricks for them (sit, shake paws, roll over—though only partway) and jumped all over Captain Winslow's boots, which made Mother quite upset, but Captain Winslow only laughed. We had a great feast with roast pork (not Ophelia!) and plum preserves and sweet potatoes. Mother played the melodeon and we all sang and it was so jolly. Mother gave the Winslows one of our goats, for the children have had no milk, for which they were so grateful it was quite something to see. They wanted to give us everything they had in return, even the two children (although that would have quite defeated the purpose of the goat).

The Winslows have been out two years now but have not had a very good season. They expect to be out another year at least. There is a good chance that we shall meet up with them again on the Sandwich Islands, and I dearly hope so, for I had so much fun playing with Content and Robin and they were both so fond of me they cried when it was time to part. Willie would have enjoyed their company, and it made me sad to think of him so far away. I hope he is quite safe and his health is good. Mother worries about him all the time, and though I pretend I don't, in truth I do. It has been so long since we have had any news of home and it scares me to realize that anything could have happened and we would not know of it. How I look forward to reaching the Sandwich Islands and I hope that there shall be letters there waiting from you.

Your wistful (a word I have wanted to use for a long time but never before had the opportunity to do so—isn't it a lovely word?) cousin,

Celia

January 27, 1857

My Dear Abigail,

I begin with terrible news. I've just discovered that the plan is to leave me behind with Mother on the Sandwich Islands while Papa goes off on the Arctic route! This is too cruel! To be abandoned with Mother all those months—think of it! And think, too, of poor Papa, alone, without us all that time. I can't understand it one bit. I am sure it is all Mother's doing because she enjoys so much the society of the Sandwich Islands. A lot of whaling wives board there while their husbands do the Northern route. I told Papa that if Mother preferred to stay behind to have tea with other ladies that was fine for her, but I would rather go with him.

"I'm afraid, my dear, that is not possible," he said. "Though I would dearly love your company, your mother needs you more."

"Mother will have plenty of society and I am sure I would be much happier with you."

"I'm afraid we can't always do what will make us happier," he said, "though I wish that were the case."

I'm sure Papa would like to have me along, but Mother won't allow it because she doesn't trust me on the ship without being there to oversee my behavior. She thinks Papa too soft and fears he would give me license to do things she never would allow.

I told Papa that if he took me, I promise I would be perfectly reformed, I would be a model of decorum. I would be marvelously polite to Mr. Grimes and not make faces behind his back. I would not abuse Isaac's kindness and have him do me all sorts of favors. I would be dignified with Nate and not laugh loudly at his jokes or engage him in races on deck. I would do all my tasks without a single argument and hem a mountain of bedsheets that Mother set aside for me and practice all the boring exercises on the melodeon, conjugate all my Latin verbs, and read the dullest Scripture. Anything.

"I will prove myself altogether worthy of you," I said.

Papa smiled and hugged me and sighed. But still he said, "Alas, I'm afraid I cannot take you along this time."

I did the best I could with pleading (and I am quite an expert at that as you well know), but still no luck. There's no appealing to Mother. She has her mind quite made up. She believes it inappropriate for a girl to be alone on a ship without a mother's protection and governance. Oh, dear Abigail, how shall I stand being stuck on the Sandwich Islands alone with Mother for so long. It is too hard!

I shall not give up prevailing upon Papa, though. Although he says the matter is settled, perhaps there's still some hope. I wonder, though, if there is some other reason they are not telling me about. They talk sometimes about matters which they do not share with me.

Your miserable cousin,
Celia

February 4, 1857

Dearest Abigail,

I shall never use the word "terrible" again for such a mild complaint. What is terrible is what I write of now.

I could not write about it for a while. I kept trying to push the scene from my mind, to stop seeing it happening again and again. But it kept coming back till I wanted to scream and run far away. You can't outrun what is troubling your mind.

The day began with such exciting prospects. A school of sperm whales close by us soon after breakfast. All the boats were lowered. Isaac's was the first one out, Papa's last. It was such a clear and sunny day, the seas so calm, the whales so close, I almost wished I could go along, for I wanted so to see firsthand what it would be like. I could count the whales—there were five—and I thought if we got them all, that would bring us more than one quarter of the way to fill our casks, and thus one quarter of the way closer to coming back home.

What foolish hopes! I was too greedy in my wishes. For instead of five whales reduced to oil in our barrels, we got no whales at all, and lost one man. It was Joseph Sylva (his full name, I learned, was Manuel Joseph de Sylveira), the boatsteerer with the wonderful, deep singing voice. His drowned body was brought up on the deck. I ran below and would not look. He was sewn in sailcloth and I came back on deck for the service. Papa read some prayers and the men all sang, and then

Joseph Sylva's body was committed to the sea. That is what is terrible, that is what the word "terrible" means. To be drowned at sea and instead of a burial in earth, to have the very sea that killed you be your final resting place!

And what is terrible is a sperm whale, thrashing and leaping through the waves, its giant flukes slamming the water. Joseph Sylva, who was boatsteerer in Isaac's boat, had thrown his harpoon and struck the whale, when it roared up and turned and came crashing down upon them. It stove the boat. The men were tossed up into the air, thrown into the sea. Papa's boat and Nate's boat raced to the rescue, but Mr. Grimes, I later learned, was in pursuit of another whale and would not command his boat back. He says he didn't realize that aid was needed, but Papa believes he ignored the cries for help and was too eager to catch a whale instead. He did not catch one. Mother ordinarily would take his side, but defers to Papa on this. Maybe now she will see Mr. Grimes better for what he is.

Papa's boat rescued Isaac and another man. Nate's boat rescued three men, but they could not get to Joseph Sylva in time. Dear Isaac was injured. His arm was badly wrenched, his leg cut by a piece of wood from the stoven boat. But he cares nothing for himself and thinks only of the man who was lost and blames himself, though there was nothing he could have done. Mr. Grimes is sullen. Papa said, "On this ship we put men before oil," and that was all. I pray that Papa will dismiss Mr. Grimes when we reach the Sandwich Islands or that he will find another berth, though I would hate to think of him being the master of a ship and having all those men under his heartless command.

Joseph Sylva was originally from Fayal, in the Azores, but even the other Portuguese on board know nothing more of him. Mother would write to his family if she could find out who they are. There may be a sweetheart waiting for him to return, or maybe a wife, or even a daughter, too. Now his body is somewhere in the ocean—what the sharks have left behind—for that is the most horrible thing, the sharks won't leave anything for long!

All those sperm whales out there, but Papa will have none of them. He is sick at heart and has given all the men a day off. But it is no holiday. This ship is like a graveyard. Even Nate looks as if he will never smile again. Mother has taken to her bed. Papa, who is the ship's doctor, has dressed Isaac's wound and I have done my best to comfort him, but he is so desolate I think even Hannah could not ease his grief.

I hate this voyage. I hate the sea. I hate these whales and I want us to kill every one of them in sight.

I have nothing more to write. I am written out.

Your poor cousin,
Celia

February 19, 1857

My Dearest Abigail,

It's there, right in front of us, land, green land, the greenest land you've ever seen. And yet we are still here on board ship, with sea between us, and may be so for hours, even days, because there is no wind! I feel as if my arm were long enough I could stretch across and reach that shore—I ache to touch that greenness.

Yet we are stuck here, not moving, not moving an inch. It isn't fair to see land after so long and to have it dangled just out of reach. I would stand on the yardarm and blow on the sail if that would help. I would ask the whole crew to blow on the sails!

Papa laughs at my impatience. "We'll be there soon enough," he says. How maddening! Soon enough? Soon enough is now, and not a minute later.

We'll be staying in Honolulu, a real town, with streets and houses and shops. Yes, shops! And horses and carriages and lots of people—ladies and other girls! Best of all, we shall get our mail from home. And I shall hear from you. (I'm sure that you have written to me, and any ship except a whaler would have beaten us to the Sandwich Islands with your letter.) It will be like listening to your sweet voice and we shall learn all the news from home.

I look forward to letters, but Mother is anxious about them. How different she and I are. Yet I understand how she fears bad news. She worries so about Willie, his safety and his health. She worries about Grandmother and Grandpa and her sister and her brothers and their families and all our friends and neighbors.

Mother has been doing poorly lately. She is tired much of the time and doesn't come up on deck too often. She has trouble climbing up the companionway. When I ask her if there is something wrong with her, she insists she's fine, yet I still feel uneasy. Since we came in sight of land, though, she seems a little better, and I am hoping she will be all recovered once we are in town. She has been busy getting our clothes in order, our trunks all packed. She frets about the fashions now in Honolulu, what the other whaling wives will be wearing. As for me, I don't care a bit, all I care about is being on land, at last.

Papa will stay with us for a few days in Honolulu

to outfit the ship and do business, but then he will leave us there. Oh, Abigail, how shall I bear it? Nate and Isaac will be gone as well. (Nate says that he will desert the ship and make his life forever in Lahaina, the port of Maui, one of the Sandwich Islands where he's been before, but I trust he is just teasing me.)

I overheard Papa and Mother talking about Mr. Grimes finding another position, and I hope that's true. Papa believes he is a competent seamen but doesn't trust him fully anymore. It scares me to think of Papa going off to the Northern Grounds with Mr. Grimes aboard, for while Mr. Grimes has shown Papa due respect so far, he's clearly no friend to Isaac and no friend to Nate. Mr. Prater is afraid of Mr. Grimes and told Papa he heard that on a previous voyage Mr. Grimes got great pleasure out of lashing the crew for small offenses. Papa said he could not believe the captain would allow it, but Mr. Prater said the captain was overly fond of his bottle and too often not on his feet to look after the running of the ship.

I go. I want this letter sealed and ready so I can post it to you as soon as we are in town. The next letter I write, dear Abigail, shall be after I read one of yours.

Pray for wind!

Your wind-lorn cousin,
Celia

February 23, 1857

Dear Abigail,

No letter from you! After all this waiting, all this looking forward to, and not a single letter! How could it be that you haven't written to me in all this time? I've written you a dozen letters, more, and not a one from you!

Yet I can't believe you wouldn't write. I can't believe that once I was gone you forgot me completely. It must be that you did write and your letters haven't reached me yet. Mother got only one letter, a brief one from Grandmother written just after we left with no real news in it at all, and so she worries, still.

It took me a day to get my land legs back. And even now I keep expecting the earth to tilt and roll like the deck of our dear ship. We're staying in a boardinghouse run by a Mrs. Farnsworth, a pleasant bedroom and sitting room that seem, after all those months in such tiny quarters, quite magnificent to me. The town is so large and noisy, I'm not sure I can get used to it—all these people, people everywhere. We have done nothing but call on other ladies and they on us, and our trunks aren't even unpacked yet!

There is a Mrs. Doane here with her daughter, Jerusha, who Mother thinks would make a suitable companion for me. She seems like a stuck-up creature to me (you should have seen the way she looked me over and though she said not one word about my dress, the curve of her lip told all), and I can't imagine we will be friends. Mother knew Mrs. Doane from her last voyage here, and they made a great show of being glad to see each other.

Mrs. Doane is an ample woman (ample being Mother's word, I would call her gargantuan) with no neck and pouches of flesh under her eyes. (Jerusha's eyes resemble hers, the pouches not so pronounced.) She looks like a slow, acquiescent sort of woman, but in fact she has a nervous disposition and bustles around with great energy, her tongue the most energetic organ of all. I would guess there is very little she is acquiescent about.

Papa has been busy doing ship's business. The crew has all gone wild to be on shore, and I gather they are not behaving themselves as Mother hoped they would. I saw Nate go flying by on a horse, and no more of him. Isaac has been buying trinkets to send to his Hannah.

I close this letter now. I am so filled with disappointment at not hearing from you that it is hard to write.

—Celia

February 26, 1857

My Very Dearest Abigail,

How unfair I was! How wrong to doubt you! I got two of your letters yesterday and you make mention of an earlier one, which I did not receive.

I read the first letter like a starving girl gobbling bread and then was angry at myself for devouring it so quickly, so I took hours for the other one, parceling it out a sentence at a time, making it last as long as I could. I've read the first one now a hundred times over, as well.

Mother got letters, too, from your mother and from Grandmother, and one from Willie, though it was clear that your mother had sat him down and made him write and done her best to correct his spelling and clean up his blotches. Willie's letter had all three of us—Papa and Mother and me—laughing out loud, and crying, too, because we miss him so, though Mother does agree he is far better off there with you, running around with his cousins, than underfoot on a small ship, getting into trouble all the time. Mother was so relieved to hear that he is healthy still, yet points out these letters were written so long ago and so much may have happened since! (I for one will enjoy this moment, as if these letters were written yesterday.)

You did not say what Sam was doing on the smoke-house roof (should I guess that our Willie dared him to climb up on there?). How terrified you must have been to think him dead when Willie called. To think he asked for grapes (of all things!) when he came to!

Your new dress sounds lovely—and yes, I do think red suits you. Of course with your complexion any color looks good on you. Mother, as you know, alas, favors brown for me (to match my eyes, she says). She thinks red makes me look sallow—but sallow I don't look after all these months at sea! (Mother would have me keep my face out of the sun, but it's impossible to do so with the wind blowing your bonnet all about, and besides the sun—when there is sun—feels so good!) I saw some absolutely beautiful blue silk in a shop here, just the color of your eyes, and shall buy it for you as a present if I can. The shops are filled with all kinds of things and it is hard to choose. I bought a tiny tea set, little cups with yellow flowers, and a dear little teapot (it will hold just a cup of tea), and a set of miniature spoons. We shall have our dolls to the most elegant tea party ever!

I accompanied Isaac when he went shopping for gifts for his Hannah. It was sweet of him to want to consult with me about what she might like best. Isaac would buy her everything in Honolulu, but since he is not a wealthy man he must do more looking than buying. He agonizes over every purchase. A mere fan he dreams about, imagining her hand holding it.

Other members of our crew are spending their

money on less noble causes, in spite of Papa's little talk on temperance, and all the work of the missionaries who try to keep liquor from these islands and keep the native young women from becoming whalemen's sweethearts. Because Papa is concerned about the behavior of his crew he wants to cut his shore leave and get back to sea, which means he shall soon be gone, and Mother and I left here alone!

Mother is tired all the time and barely wants to leave our rooms. She assures me there is nothing to worry about, and yet I do. Mrs. Doane and her despicable daughter have taken me under their wing. Jerusha thinks herself better than the rest of the world because her papa's made a fortune. She's been here several times before, and always stays in the finest guest house and knows everything there is to know about the Sandwich Islands and tells you so, whether you want to listen or not. I don't know how I can stand her more, yet Mother thinks she is the perfect companion for me! I would rather have a dozen of the roughest seamen to talk to than Miss Jerusha Doane of Orient Point, Long Island. This morning Toby was chewing on the edge of her skirt while she was talking at me. She did not notice and I did not point it out to her.

Your happy-to-hear-from-you cousin,
Celia

added later

Mr. Grimes just reported to Papa that Nate was in a drunken brawl which he claims Nate instigated and got beaten up, which he believes Nate deserved. He wants him dismissed immediately. Can it be? Mother says she was afraid Nate might end up involved in something like this. Papa says he must inquire of Nate the full circumstances before he decides to dismiss him.

February 28, 1857

Dearest Abigail,

Even another letter from you could not cheer me up. Papa is to sail tomorrow. He is going south, for a short cruise, a month or so, and will stop by here again before he goes to the Northern Grounds for a longer tour. I think he is worried because Mother is not well and he does not want to be gone now for long. I cannot bear to think of him leaving us here. It will be so dreadful without him. Mother is tired and crabby and sends me off with that annoying Mrs. Doane and her horrid daughter, Jerusha.

Mr. Grimes gave false report against Nate. He claims he was only repeating what had been told to him by a mate on the *Islip*. Fortunately Papa spoke to other witnesses and learned that the brawl Nate was involved in was not his fault at all, in fact he acted with great bravery, going to the defense of William Greene, one of our Portuguese, who had gotten into a fight with a seaman from the *Islip* over (I am not supposed to know this, but I do) a native lady. Nate dove into the battle when a knife was pulled and Thomas did not have one. I saw Nate only briefly. His eye is all purple and his lip is swollen so he looks like he got stung by bees. But even so, he is the most beautiful of men and I shall miss him sorely.

Mr. Grimes has not found another place and so is staying with our ship. I am not surprised that no one else would want him. I wish Papa were to sing his praises so that someone else would snap him up, but Papa is too honest for that. I heard Mother say to Papa, "I'm sure he will not cause you trouble, Daniel," but it was said with more hope than conviction.

Papa has hired on two Kanakas (natives of the Sandwich Islands). One is to take the place of Joseph Sylva. (What man, though, can truly take the place of another?) This man has a smooth, round, friendly-looking face, and Papa was told he is a fine whale-man—yet can he sing those velvety deep notes? The other is to take the place of a whaleman, Jed Peal, who has deserted. There's been a reward posted for his return, but no sign of him. Desertion is a crime, for all these men have signed the ship's articles, yet I can see how one might want to stay here on this green and luxurious island rather than get back on board the ship.

I hope tomorrow never comes!

Your saddest cousin,
Celia

March 2, 1857

Dearest Abigail,

Papa is gone. I watched the ship in the distance until I could no longer see the speck it had become, and then I kept my eyes on that same spot on the horizon where it had disappeared. How can it disappear so completely and yet still exist?

Nothing here pleases me now. I don't care for land, or green, or town. All I want is to be on board the *Jupiter* again with Papa and Nate and Isaac. It is one thing to leave one's home (I have done that) and quite another to have one's home sail away, grow smaller and smaller, and get swallowed up by distance. How strange it is, Abigail, that a month ago I could not wait to leave the *Jupiter*, and now it seems the dearest place on earth to me. It's all a matter of being with those you love.

We had a dozen callers come to cheer us up. I had to stay and be polite. The only thing that was the least bit cheering was to hear that the *Ranger* is nearing port and we shall soon get to see the Winslows. I can't wait to see Robin and Content. The annoying Mrs. Doane and the detestable Jerusha stayed the whole time. I would not cry in front of Jerusha. They invited me on an outing tomorrow, but I said I did not choose to go. Mrs. Doane is not one to take rejection lightly.

"We shall come by for you in case you change your mind," she said.

"I won't," I said.

Mother was angry at me for what she calls my impertinence and for rejecting such a kind offer. "You were rude and disrespectful," she told me.

"I wasn't rude, I was only honest," I said. "I won't change my mind, and it was only right that I say so."

"What is the matter with you? Why don't you want to go with them?" she asked me.

"Nothing is the matter with me," I said. "It's simply that I don't enjoy their company."

"But Jerusha is so close to you in age, and such a charming young lady, so well brought up."

"Charming! She is arrogant and self-centered—"

"That's unjust, Celia," said Mother. "And in any case, you must always look at a person's good qualities. Remember, we are far from home and our family and dearest friends, and must be grateful for the company we have. It's time you learned to make allowances."

"You don't understand anything!" I said. And I ran outside and down the street and down towards the harbor so I could cry in peace. I wanted to jump aboard a ship and follow Papa. Oh, that I could do that! I wanted never to go back to that sitting room in that boardinghouse. But of course I did, because I could hardly wander long on the streets alone.

When I got back, Mother looked as if she had been weeping. I am sure she is sad, as I am, about Papa leaving. I would have sought her arms for an embrace, but she said, "I have been waiting for you for tea," and all my anger rose up inside me once again. I said, "I'm not having tea, so go ahead without me," and went to my room. I was sorry then, because Mother's face looked so sad, but it is not all my own fault, is it?

And so we sat, two miserable women in two separate rooms. There is no comfort to be had.

Oh, Abigail, this time with Papa away shall be interminable!

Your miserable cousin,
Celia

March 3, 1857

Dearest Abigail,

Mother has been in bed all day. She says she is just tired from all the preparations for Papa's leaving, but she looks so pale and weak I fear there's something worse. I was wrong to run off yesterday evening, then refuse to have tea with her.

Mrs. Doane and Jerusha came by this morning, as they had threatened to do. I still said I would not go with them on their excursion.

"I suppose it's best," said Mrs. Doane. "Your mother needs you." But I have been cornered into promising I would go with them on some small outing they have planned for tomorrow.

What if Mother gets very ill while Papa is away? What shall I do?

What if she dies?

—Celia

March 4, 1857

Dearest Abigail,

Now I know. And now you shall know all, too.

I hate Jerusha even more than I did before.

They came for me soon after breakfast this morning

and had a carriage all waiting and a picnic lunch all packed. Mrs. Doane is nothing if not efficient. She had placed the picnic basket on the seat beside her, so I was stuck riding backwards, next to Jerusha. Jerusha acted as if she was bored with the whole expedition—of course she has seen these falls a hundred times before—but was going along to please me. Such kindness!

The falls were quite magnificent and took my breath away. I could tell that it was difficult for Jerusha to keep pretending she was bored because they are the sort of falls that even if you've seen them as many times as she has, they would still take your breath away again. Mrs. Doane encountered another visitor there, a Mrs. Thackeray, another one of her "dearest friends." As they moved slower than we along the walk, I was stuck making conversation with Jerusha.

And so that's when I found out. Jerusha was talking about Mrs. Doane's work with the missionary ladies in Lahaina. "She'd have your mother join her there later in the spring, but of course your mother will be occupied with the baby then."

"Baby?" I said, stupidly, for I wasn't paying close attention to her. "Why, Willie's not coming over to join us. And he's no baby. He's eight years old."

"I meant the new baby, of course," she said to me. In a second everything came clear. I could not say a word, but everything was there on my face.

Jerusha put her hand up to her mouth as if to stifle her words, and said, coyly, "Oh dear, I suppose I shouldn't have said anything, should I?"

So of course I had to pretend that I had known all along. I could not have her knowing something about my family that I did not know myself.

Mrs. Doane came waddling up then, with Mrs. Thackeray, and said to me, "Isn't this the most spectacular of views, my dear?"

"Yes," I answered. But the view, the falls, everything was spoiled for me. I will never be able to think of that place again without remembering the smug look on Jerusha's face and the way I felt discovering that Mother and Papa had kept this news a secret from me.

So Mother isn't ill, has not been all this time. It is just that a baby is expected. Why did I have to find out from Jerusha (who must have overheard her mother speak of it)? Why couldn't they have told me?!

I miss you Abigail! I need someone to talk to and there's no one here.

Your cousin,
Celia

March 6, 1857

Dearest Abigail,

The Winslows have arrived, thank goodness, and I have been spared the constant company of the ladies from Orient Point, Long Island. The Winslows were exuberantly happy to see us, and Content and Robin hugged me and danced around with joy. They took me riding with them today and it was quite a lark. Captain Winslow is big for even the biggest horse. He is a wild and jovial rider. He flew off his horse while taking a fence at a gallop and just got himself up, laughed, and hoisted his portly body back into the saddle again. Mary Winslow rides more cautiously, but Robin and Content are just like their father. Content rides like a man, with her legs astride the horse, as the native women do here. Jerusha would be horrified.

Mother said that she was planning to tell me about the baby very soon and was sorry that I learned the news from Jerusha. She does not understand why I am upset that she told Mrs. Doane before me. Mother says she won't write to Grandmother or your mother about the baby coming; she will wait until the baby is born, since news travels so slowly and she does not want to worry them. So what I have written to you is a secret you must keep.

We have now embarked on a project of making

baby clothes. It is more interesting than hemming sheets, but the clothing is tiny and Mother requires my stitches be tiny, too. I shall be cross-eyed before we're done.

Mother frets constantly about Papa's return. She does not expect the baby to be born for another month at least, but she is anxious that Papa be back in time. I long to have him back myself!

I got your sweetest letter yesterday and have been carrying it around with me all day, reading it in little bits to myself. It is so strange to think of snow while here it is so hot my hand is sore with fanning myself.

I can't believe that Eliza Chipman would want to engage herself to Mr. Soames. He has such a large nose, and hands, and feet! Surely she could marry someone more exciting, but at least a schoolmaster is planted on terra firma and won't be abandoning her to chase whales in distant seas. I think often how poor Hannah must be missing her Isaac.

I do not know that any of my letters have reached you yet. I pray they have. The one advantage of being marooned here is that ships carry mail back home fairly often, so I have some faith you'll get a letter soon.

Your affectionate cousin,
Celia

My dear, dear Abigail,

The baby was born today. A baby girl. Very frail, very tiny, but beautiful, with the softest, finest hair. Her skin is almost clear as window glass, and you can see all the blue veins like threads beneath the surface. She was born so much earlier than was expected and doesn't look ready to be in the world.

I was wakened in the middle of the night by Mother calling out for me. I thought she had been stricken with something terrible the way she clutched at the bed-sheets, her face was all contorted, her hair all loose.

"The baby—" she gasped. At first I didn't understand. The baby, this soon?

"Get help," she said. "It's coming."

I ran to the Winslows' rooms (they are staying in the same lodgings as we) and pounded on the door. Captain Winslow, in nightshirt, opened it. I barely had to speak—he got Mary up right away and she came running back to Mother with me. Captain Winslow ran for Mrs. Farnsworth and the doctor.

"Help me," Mother was crying, "please help me, God!" Mary grasped Mother's hand and told her the doctor was on the way. She asked me to go stay with Content and Robin, for they would be frightened to find themselves alone in the middle of the night.

"Your mother will be all right," she said. "I promise you."

I was afraid to leave, but I was afraid, also, to stay. I went back to the Winslows' rooms and lay down beside Content, but then I remembered Toby, and thought I should go fetch him, for he would get underfoot, so I went back. The door to the bedroom was closed, but I could hear Mother screaming in a high, strange voice, and I could not bear it, so I ran back to the Winslows' and got into bed again with Content. But even there I could hear Mother screaming, or thought I could.

"She's dying," I thought. "She's dying." I thought of Captain Freeman's wife, Harriet, who had died in childbirth, and Mother's cousin, Almira.

I tried to remember when Willie was born—for Mother had been all right then, but I was too young at the time and all that I could remember was trying out the cradle for myself to see how fast it would rock and Grandmother pulling me out. I was staying at your house the next time Mother had a baby (the one that was lost).

I tried to remember other things, anything to take my mind away, but I could not escape that boarding-house and Mother's pain. Content was very sweet and hugged me close. After a while she fell asleep, and her arm slipped back down beside her.

The night was hot and endless. Mother and I were on the other side of the world from home, and Papa wasn't with us. I thought Mother would never cease screaming and the baby would never be born.

"Please don't die, Mother!" I whispered. "Oh, Mother, please don't die!"

There was a figure in the doorway. It was Mary. She walked towards the bed softly and sat down beside me. She told me that Mother had given birth to a baby girl and all was well. She kissed me and stroked my hair. I listened to the rhythm of Content's breathing as she slept beside me, and Mary's soft lullaby, and finally I fell asleep.

In the morning Mother was propped up in bed with the new baby in her arms. Mother's hair had been brushed and arranged nicely high on her head. The baby looked like a wax doll, not much bigger than my doll Rebecca. I was afraid to go too close, but Mother patted the bed beside her and had me sit.

"We'll name her Sallie, your grandmother's name. Would you like that?" she asked.

"Yes," I said.

"You may hold her."

I held my arms out to take her. I was trembling so, I was afraid I could not lift her, but she weighed almost nothing.

"Hello, Sallie," I said. She did not open her eyes, but she made a little mewing sound. I thought for a moment of the new kittens we had the year before and how I had taken one and wrapped it in my doll's quilt and pretended it was a baby.

Sallie's hands were miniatures. I touched one softly with my pinky and she gripped my finger with a quick fierceness. I would have held her for hours like that, but Mother needed to try to get her to nurse.

All day long visitors came by. They all said she was a beautiful baby. Mary helped seeing people in and out and bringing tea for Mother and all the guests. She is good-humored about everything, which is what I expected, what is a surprise is to see how competent she can be, as well.

"Mary, you've had no sleep," Mother said. "You should go back to bed."

But Mary just laughed, and said, "You've had no sleep, either. And I'm just fine, I tell you, I'm just fine."

Mrs. Doane and Jerusha were among the visitors, of course. Mrs. Doane seemed more put out that she had not been the one called in the night than she was happy to see the baby.

"I was quite ready to be here at a moment's notice," she told me. She could barely bring herself to speak to Mary, who, she felt, had usurped her place. She had lots of advice about how the baby should be handled and which window should be open and what Mother should eat, but no one paid her much attention.

As they were leaving, Jerusha turned to me. "I'm sorry about the baby," she said.

"Sorry?" I asked. "Why sorry?"

"That it's so small. Mother thinks it's unlikely it will last long."

I could not think what to say. If Mary hadn't come up just then and put her arm around my shoulder, my fist might have ended up in Miss Orient Point, Long Island's face.

And so I have a sister. I do not know what to think, it has happened so suddenly, so unexpectedly. If only Papa were here! He is the father of a new daughter now and he doesn't even know! (Or do you think it's possible he somehow knows and is sailing towards us as I write?) Mother was too tired to write to him so I wrote for her and she just signed her name. She will write to Grandmother and your mother as soon as she is able, but if this letter reaches you first, you may be the one to tell the happy news to all.

Love from your exhausted cousin,
Celia

March 14, 1857

Dear Abigail,

The doctor came to look at Sallie yesterday. He had nothing encouraging to say and nothing promising to suggest. She is so frail, and barely nurses. Her skin is so white, it is almost blue. She does not cry like other babies, but only whimpers as if she does not have the strength to cry. Still, she is the most beautiful baby you ever saw; everyone who sees her says so. Oh, Abigail, I wish that you could see her too!

Mother has written several letters to Papa. There are ships departing here every day and we pray that one will meet him. I have never wanted him so desperately. I am so afraid he will not get back soon.

I remember now those three little headstones in the cemetery. The first two infants born soon after me, the third one after Willie. It never breathed at all, born way too early.

This morning Mary helped Mother get Sallie all dressed up in her fine little clothes and we had her photographed. It costs a great deal of money, but Mother felt better when it was done. We did not speak, but we both knew what the other thought.

Mrs. Doane and Jerusha visited again today, but not for long because Mother was very tired after the exertions of the morning, and, I suspect, pretended to be even more tired than she was. Mrs. Doane fussed around the room and made various comments about how things would be better managed if she were in charge, instead of "that flighty Mary Winslow." She is still put out that Mother didn't summon her for the birth, and regrets that we aren't staying in her lodgings (which she believes to be far superior to ours) so it would be more convenient for her to be in attendance. I saw them to the door.

"Mrs. Doane hopes she will be able to visit you again tomorrow," I reported to Mother when I came back in.

"Oh dear," said Mother, "I hope not!"

"I thought Mrs. Doane was your dearest friend," I said.

Mother smiled. "Eunice is a dear friend and a good woman, but in truth I far prefer having Mary's company—though she might not get things exactly right—than Eunice, who always does." Mother and I laughed together, and then she held out her arms to me. I sat on the bed beside her and laid my head against her chest and cried and cried.

"It's all right, Sweetheart," she whispered to me. "It's all right."

"I want Papa back!" I cried.

"One of my letters will surely reach him soon," she said.

"But Sallie—"

"God will do whatever is best," she said. "I am content with that."

But Abigail, how can it be best for babies to be born so frail they do not have the strength to cry?

Pray for us!

—Celia

March 16, 1857

Dear Abigail,

Sallie died yesterday. Sallie died and Papa is not back. He will never see her sweet face, he will never touch her tiny hand. Mother wanted to save a lock of her hair, but she could not bring herself to cut it. Mary took a little snip and placed it in a round gold locket which she gave Mother. It was a locket of her own and Mother did not want to take it, but at last she did.

In her coffin, Sallie looked just like a doll in a doll's box. She was wearing the white cap that I trimmed with lace and the white dress Mother made, with satin bows.

The photograph does not look like her, but it will have to do.

The chapel was crowded for the funeral. I sat with

Mother in the front. I could not really listen to one word that Mr. Prollock said. I could not wait to get out of that small, stifling building into the fresh air. At the graveyard Content held my hand. Mrs. Doane and Jerusha were there, but I did not speak with them.

It is strange to be back in our rooms now and to have nothing of the baby here. A chair stands where the cradle was beside the bed. It is as if Sallie has never been. Mother is writing letters now, as I write to you. Now you can share the news you already know, about Sallie's birth, as you share with them the sad news of her death. Willie has had a sister he never saw. Now it is just the two of us again.

Mary has come to say that Papa's ship is in the harbor. I run!

—C.

March 17, 1857

Dearest Abigail,

Papa's back!

We could see the *Jupiter* out there in the harbor, and it seemed to take forever for the whaleboat to be lowered and Papa to be rowed to the dock. He had not heard the news, but one look at Mother's face and he knew all.

We went first to our lodgings, then the graveyard. The grave was covered with flowers. Papa kneeled down and stayed very still for some time, his head bowed. He did not make a sound, but when he looked up I had to turn away. He put one arm around Mother's waist and one around mine and we walked slowly out of the graveyard, like a creature with six legs and three heads. Mother wanted to walk all the way back to our lodgings. Papa was worried that she was too weak, but she insisted, and so we did.

Here is the happy news: Papa got two whales, one a right whale, together making 190 barrels of oil.

We dined with the Winslows and Papa told us all about his time away. The second whale, a sperm whale, gave a long, rough chase. One whaleboat was overturned, but all men saved, and Papa praised the Kanaka, who is the best swimmer he has ever seen. He will take on another Kanaka while he is here, for one of the crew, a greenhand named Chalmers Taber, has been ill with a fever and will stay here on the island.

It is wonderful to have Papa back, to have him safe. I'd thought that once he had returned all would be right in the world. But nothing can be right with Sallie snatched away after so few days with us. Nothing can be perfectly all right again.

Your cousin,
Celia

March 24, 1857

Dearest Abigail,

What news! What exciting news! We are going with Papa to the Northern Grounds! It is all decided. Mother would not have wanted to take a tiny baby to the Bering Strait, but now she has no reason to stay here.

I can't wait to be on board the *Jupiter* again. I can't wait to see Nate and Isaac and all the crew (except for Mr. Grimes, of course). I will miss the Winslows and I will miss this green land, but Honolulu can never be a happy place for me.

I got your wonderful letter, and it was strange that when you wrote it you had gotten only one of mine, the earliest I wrote. You did not know then about Sallie's birth—or death. I wonder if by now you know.

I am glad to hear that Willie is thriving. (I'm sure you're reporting only the best of him.) Thank you for getting him to add a note to your letter. It couldn't have been easy to make him sit still that long and to keep him from covering the sheet with blots of ink. Please give him a long hug and remind him that his sister loves and misses him.

I end quickly to post this letter. It will be the last I can send from here. It will be months before we are back again, yet I will keep writing to you faithfully and will hope we gam with ships that are returning long before us.

Your soon-to-be-sailing-again cousin,
Celia

April 14, 1857

My Dear Abigail,

I'd forgotten what it is like! For three weeks I have been sick and wretched—utterly wretched. For three weeks I have been in my bunk, too sick to be bored, too sick to care about anything. So wretched that I even thought that I would rather have been left behind on the Sandwich Islands with Mrs. Doane and the despicable Jerusha than be aboard this ship!

Today is the first day I feel well enough to be on deck, the first time I am able to write to you since we departed. It was hard for me to climb up the companion-way, I was so weak. All those days I had not wanted to eat, and the little I managed to get down did not stay down for long.

I had thought I would never be seasick again, once I'd gotten my sea legs, but all that time on land ruined my body for the sea, and I've had to learn to get used to it all over again. It's relatively calm now (though a strong wind), but we are headed to the treacherous north, and the sea is not one to be trusted—how well I know that! I fear there is good reason so many whaling wives choose to remain behind on the Sandwich Islands while their husbands go to the Northern Grounds.

My homecoming on the *Jupiter* was a happy one at first. (I did not get struck with seasickness till we were a day out.) When I boarded the ship I ran around, checking out with pleasure my old spots—how tiny our cabins seem after our rooms in the boardinghouse!—and climbing into the waistboat (where now I sit to write). Everyone seemed so glad to have us back (except Mr. Grimes, of course), even Mr. Hodgeson, the cook, who is in reasonable spirits because now the pantry is full of fresh food. He will grow increasingly grumbly as we get farther from land and stores begin to run low.

I wanted to run and hug Nate—how I would have loved to be swept up in his arms!—but of course I did not do so. I asked him if he was happy to have us back.

"This ship was a dreary place without Toby dashing around on the deck," he said.

"And what about me?" I asked. "Didn't you miss me just a little?"

"Let's see," said Nate, grinning, "I suppose I might have."

Then I asked him if he liked my new dress and twirled around to show it best, but he pronounced it "rather grand for this old ship."

"Well, it's not for everyday, of course," I said. "But you haven't told me if you like it."

"Green's a pretty color."

"That's still not saying if you like the dress."

"If you want the truth," said Nate, "I think the dress is better suited for a matron of thirty than a girl of twelve."

I told him I would be thirteen in two days.

"Hey, now," said Nate. "No need to be hurt. You asked my opinion and I gave you an honest one. I'm not fond of dresses like that with all those—what do you call them?—flounces. And you're a pretty enough girl not to need such stuff."

"I am?" I asked.

"I better watch what I'm saying, now, hadn't I?" said Nate, laughing. "So, are we friends again?"

"Yes," I said. I would have given him a kiss, but he held out his hand and so I shook it. And wouldn't you know that was just the minute that Mr. Grimes turned up—he is always turning up when you least expect him, and when you least want him. He said nothing, but he gave me such a look, as if I did not belong there. I stared right back at him, and said nothing, either, and then I turned and went below.

Isaac got three letters from his Hannah when he was in port and showed them to me, though not to read, but just to see her fine handwriting. Sometimes, I'm told, a seaman who gets no mail will buy a letter from another crewman, but you can be sure Isaac would rather sell his own flesh. The letters were worn thin from having been read so many times. I have read your letters over and again a thousand times. It will be so long—too, too long—before I have a letter from you again. It may be months before I can send this letter on to you.

Isaac says he thinks I have grown taller on the Sandwich Islands. I wonder if he is right. I wished we had made a mark of my height when I first came aboard the ship, like the mark on the wall by the staircase at home.

"We'll do it now," said Isaac, "and then see if you grow taller in the Bering Sea."

And so he took a pencil and marked right on the wall and wrote the date (which is not easy to do on a rolling ship). Now we must remember to check again in a few months' time.

Mr. Prater, the steward, was happy to have Mother back. Although he has two more persons to take care of with us on board, Mother does much of the looking after Papa. "The Captain is a more melancholy man when you're not around," he said, and that wrenched my heart to think of Papa all those weeks without us on board. How lonely he must have been, worrying about Mother and whether the baby was born.

We don't talk about Sallie much. We made a last visit to her grave before we left. There is a tiny headstone there with Sallie's name and dates and underneath it says:

Sleep on sweet babe and take your rest.
To call you home God saw it best.

Mrs. Farnsworth said she would go every week and leave flowers there. Mother cried to be leaving her baby behind in a foreign land.

"I will never do that again," she said. "I will never bury someone I love anywhere but in our cemetery at home."

I don't know how that could be possible, though, if someone died far from home, but I did not say anything. In any case, being buried in a real churchyard in real ground, even if it is far away, is so much better than being buried at sea. And Sallie has a pretty grave. And the island is so fair—with sunshine and greenness.

But poor, sweet little Sallie, left alone, left behind. And now we are sailing far off without her and it is as if she never was.

I hated to part with the Winslows, and Mother did, too.

"I will never forget all you've done for us," said Mother. "I didn't have my mother or my sister here to comfort me, but God was good to me by granting me your friendship." She clasped her locket in her hand. "I can never thank you enough for this," she said, "for now it is all I have of her."

Mother and Mary held each other and cried, and Content and Robin hugged me and cried, and even Captain Winslow had tears rolling down his plump, pink cheeks. They are like our family, now. I hope it will not be too long before we see them again. If their ship's repairs are done in time, they will be coming to the Northern Grounds as well.

The problem with the Northern Grounds is that the season there is short. Summer is barely over before the sea starts freezing and you have to be sure to head back south soon enough so your ship does not get caught in the ice. I heard Captain Winslow talk to Papa about it. The ice would break the ship apart, and even if it didn't, you could not survive the Arctic winter if you were trapped there.

How I wish we were homeward bound now, not sailing off to a place I've never been, farther away from home than ever before!

There are supposed to be great numbers of bowhead whales in the Bering Sea. And if that is so, and if we can catch many, maybe we can fill our barrels and then, oh then, at last, maybe we can head straight back home!

Your cousin Celia,

At sea again

April 15, 1857

Dear Abigail,

I had so much to write in the last letter that I neglected to tell you about my birthday. I would have forgotten about it entirely, because on the 27th I was too seasick to think of anything at all, except that Mother and Papa remembered. They gave me a lacquered sewing box from Japan, with little trays and compartments all cleverly arranged inside and outfitted with spindles and spools and needles all finely carved in ivory. I was not able to admire it till now. We had no celebration because I was too wretched to get up from my bunk. There was cake, but I could not bear to even look at it. I hope this is my last birthday at sea!

I thought being thirteen would feel quite different from being twelve—it certainly sounds much older—but it does not feel different in the least. I'm afraid I don't look any older, either.

Your cousin,
Celia

P.S. Nate is nineteen (I know this from Papa), though the crew believes him to be twenty.

April 28, 1857

Dear Abigail,

I used to find Mr. Grimes merely distasteful, but now he frightens me. He sneaks around the ship as if he is on the lookout for something. He has taken up a friendship (I say friendship but it does not deserve such a sweet term) with the ship's cooper, Hiram Beck, a nasty little man with a weasel's face and a notched lip so you see his side tooth even when his mouth is closed.

I told Papa I feared they were up to something. I had expected him to laugh and tell me there was nothing for me to worry about, but he said, "I'll keep my eye on them," so now I am truly concerned. I shall talk to Nate, too—if we ever have a chance to be alone—for I know Mr. Grimes has always wished him harm, and was disappointed that his attempt to get Nate dismissed was unsuccessful.

Oh, Abigail, to be stuck on board a ship with such a man!

—Celia

May 12, 1857

My Dearest Abigail,

I had such a dream last night! I dreamed that I was holding Sallie in my arms, but she seemed so still and would not stir even when I shook her a little, and when I looked down it was my doll Rebecca I was holding, instead. I kept shaking her and tapping her, but she would not become Sallie again. I started screaming and

Mother came running in—we were in our house, in Eastham—and I dropped the doll and Mother snatched her up and it was Sallie she was holding and she was rocking her back and forth and Sallie was whimpering in that little way she had.

I did not tell Mother about my dream, it would upset her so. But this evening I was on deck with Papa and I told him. He took me in his arms and hugged me and I cried and cried.

"I prayed for Sallie, Papa," I said, "and Mother did, too. But we lost her anyway. Why didn't God listen? If God's merciful and kind, how can he let babies die? And how can he let men drown in the sea? Mother says that God does things for the best, but how can such things be for the best?"

"I can't answer that," he said, sadly.

"Do you believe God listens to our prayers?"

Papa sighed. "I don't have the same kind of faith your mother does. I think God leaves a lot up to us to work out for ourselves."

"So what's the good of prayers?"

"Prayers"—and Papa smiled a little—"prayers can be a comfort, sometimes. But you can't rely on them."

"What can you rely on, then?"

"The only thing you can rely on is yourself, and the people you love."

I looked out at the sea. It was so grey and cold. There was nothing but sea as far as the eye could reach.

Papa put his arm around my shoulder.

"I don't worry about you, Celia," he said. "God has made you smart and resourceful and courageous. Trust in yourself."

Oh, Abigail, how I wish that praying always worked!

I'd pray that Sallie be restored to us, that I'd pick up my doll in my arms and she would turn into real Sallie again.

I'd pray our casks were full of oil.

I'd pray that we were heading home.

No whales for so long. The crew is getting restless. Everyone is feeling dreary. Everyone is in a crabby temper, Mr. Prater murmurs all the time, and even Nate doesn't whistle anymore.

—Celia

May 23, 1857

Dearest Abigail,

No whales. No whales. What shall we do?

We gammed with another ship, the *Orlando* out of Sag Harbor. The Captain, Uriah Cushman, has come from the North where we are headed and has not done well there. He is trying his luck elsewhere. Were all the reports Papa got false ones?

Captain Cushman's wife, Dorothea, is at least twenty years younger than he, and this is her bridal voyage. The Captain is quite besotted with her, and every other sentence out of his mouth is an inquiry about her welfare—*"Are you quite comfortable my dear?"*—or a reference to her wishes—*"Dorothea likes tea served at exactly four o'clock, whenever possible."* If they spend another year together he shall be left with no opinions of his own whatsoever. He has had a little deckhouse built for her so she can sit inside in inclement weather and not have to go below. Mother was quite taken with it—and I also—and so Papa has asked the ship's carpenter to build one for us. Won't that be nice?

I came across Isaac last evening standing at the railings and I am sure that he had been crying, although he did his best to wipe his face and try to look as if that were not the case.

I gently touched his arm. "Don't worry, Isaac," I said. "We'll be heading back to the Sandwich Islands soon enough and there will be more letters from Hannah waiting for you."

Isaac only nodded.

"And it won't be that long," I continued, "before we are heading home and then you'll marry Hannah!"

"If she waits for me."

"Of course she'll wait for you, Isaac."

"What a life this is, Celia!"

"What life would you wish for, then?" I asked him.

"A farmer's life. A house, a barn, a field, a horse, some cows. My wife beside me."

"But wouldn't that be dull after some time? Wouldn't you miss whaling and the sea?"

"If that be dull, then dull is what I crave. Whaling is just a way to earn a living—it's what my family's always done, it's what I know how to do. But if I had a house and some land, I'd be content to never see the sea again."

I told him he would get his house and land, and it wouldn't be very long before he made his fortune. And in the meantime, when he was a captain, and that would be someday soon, he could take Hannah on his voyages with him.

"If she'd come," he said.

"Of course she'd come. My mother comes."

"Your mother is a most extraordinary woman," said Isaac. "She puts up with a great deal of hardship to accompany your father on his voyages."

I'd never heard anyone call Mother an extraordinary woman before. I would have explained to Isaac Mother's true reason for sailing with Papa—the story of Papa's first wife, Demaris—but I could not breach Nate's confidence.

What shall we do if we find no whales? Perhaps they have all been hunted and there are none left. Perhaps they have gotten very smart and know how to elude all the whaleships; while we search their old grounds, they go somewhere new. The ocean is so vast, so endless, they could hide anywhere.

Your cousin,
Celia

May 28, 1857

Dear Abigail,

A terrible fight on board yesterday. It was a rare, sunny afternoon, warm enough for me to take my perch in the waistboat, my favorite reading spot. Four men were playing cards out on the deck and I looked up when I heard them shouting. It was the carpenter, the blacksmith, that weasel-faced cooper, Hiram Beck, and a boatsteerer, named Charlie McFarlane, who Papa says is "a nimble seaman but a scamp."

The cooper accused Charlie of cheating—which I have every reason to believe he may have done—and Charlie hotly denied it, sprang up, and upset the cards. The cooper called him names which I would be reluctant to put into writing (even if I could spell them, which I am not sure I can) and then Charlie threatened him with his fist, for which he got a shove in return. Then they were at it. The carpenter and the blacksmith began by trying to pull them apart but got struck themselves which made them so angry they joined in the fight, the blacksmith siding with the cooper, the carpenter with Charlie, and they were all four pounding each other and rolling on the deck. No one saw me watching, though I had an excellent view from the waistboat, and no one heard me call for help. It was strange because although I did not want to watch (faces were bloodied and it was a gruesome sight) I could not draw my eyes away.

The cooper, who was getting the worst of it from Charlie, pulled a knife. Charlie saw it just in time and grabbed a piece of wood and clobbered him. The knife went flying across the deck. At that moment Isaac came running up and Mr. Grimes soon after. The four men were pulled apart, a bloody, panting mass, and order was restored. Isaac caught a glimpse of me watching from the waistboat and with his hand signaled for me to duck down, which I did. I could no longer see what was going on, but I could hear it all.

When Papa came up on deck, Nate just behind him, Mr. Grimes presented him with a description of the event, laying full blame on Charlie, claiming it was he who drew the knife. Fighting is not tolerated on the ship, and drawing a knife is a most serious offense. Papa pronounced punishment—chores on deck and extra watches for all the men involved in the fight, and Charlie he commanded to be put in irons and be brought below. How that chilled my heart. I could not help peeping up over the edge of the boat. Charlie's face was wild with anger and fear. There was blood dripping out of the corner of his mouth where a tooth had been knocked out. I felt dizzy trying to decide what to do.

"It was not my knife, sir, I never touched it!" cried Charlie.

"Be still, young man!" shouted Mr. Grimes. "If this were my ship I would have you flogged not just for your crime but for insubordination."

Suddenly, without thinking, I found myself standing up in the boat.

"Papa," I said, "what Charlie says is true. It was Mr. Beck who drew the knife."

Everyone turned to look at me.

"What is she doing here?" snarled Mr. Grimes.

"Celia," Papa asked me, "have you been there all this time?" He lifted me out of the boat (though I could certainly climb down myself) and set me on deck.

"I've been here the last hour, Papa," I said. "I saw it all."

"And what did you see?"

And so I told him, just as I told you, how the fight progressed.

Papa picked up the knife and held it before the cooper.

"Do you deny that this is yours?" he asked him.

Mr. Beck would not speak.

"All you have against him is the word of a child," said Mr. Grimes.

"I will deal with this matter, thank you, Mr. Grimes," said Papa. He told the men to go to their duties, he told Isaac to accompany me to our quarters, and he told Mr. Beck he wanted a word with him in private.

"Are you all right, Celia?" asked Isaac, for I was shaking so.

"I think I am," I said.

"Well, you're certainly not a meek young lady," said Isaac, smiling somewhat. "What will your mother say?"

Mother, as you can expect, was horrified that I had interfered in the business of the ship, and put myself in a position of bearing witness against one of the crew.

"I saw what happened, Mother, I saw it all!"

"But you should not have spoken out the way you did."

"I couldn't just stand by and allow Charlie to be convicted of something he didn't do."

Later Papa joined us. "It was a rash thing you did, Celia," he said. But then he turned to Mother. "This is our fault, entirely, Ann. We raised our daughter to be not only honest but courageous. I'm not sure we would have her not be so."

"But what about her own welfare?" asked Mother. "Hiram Beck, even in irons, is not a man whose enmity I want to arouse."

"I have not put him in irons, for that very reason," said Papa. "I told him I would let him off this time, for I knew he had been provoked, but told him if he ever wielded a knife again he would lose his position on my ship."

But it's Mr. Grimes I fear even more now than the cooper. He knows I know he lies. And no man likes having his faults revealed, especially by someone he dismisses as a child.

Papa says the reason for the fight is that the crew is all demoralized. It has been so long since we have seen a whale. When there are whales to be chased, the whaleman's life is a dangerous one. When there are whales to be rendered, the whaleman's life is a hard one. But when there is neither, the whaleman's life is a boring one, and of the three it is that the men hate most.

Please, Abigail, pray for whales!

Your cousin,
Celia

June 17, 1857

Dear Abigail,

I am sitting in our cabin now, all cozy and warm by the woodstove, feeling as happy as I have been on this trip so far, the source of which I shall go into greater detail later. Mother and Papa are both engaged in reading. Toby, after his strenuous day, is curled up asleep at my feet. He is dreaming doggy dreams, and every now and then yips as if he is in pursuit of something. You would almost mistake us for a family in a real parlor in a real house, sitting by the woodstove on a winter's eve. (June in the Arctic can be like winter.)

I haven't written to you for many days, but there hasn't been much to write before this. We made good speed heading north, but saw no whales. If I wrote every day, every day I would have written the same thing: no whales. No whales.

It has been very dull except for the time I spend with Papa doing the navigation. Papa thinks I am so good at it now, he has me take my sights, consult the tables, and do the calculations all by myself. When clouds cover the sun and moon and stars and I can get no observations, he has me be the one to work time and figure our position. (It takes two of us to measure our rate of sailing, one to turn the sand-glass and one to handle the log-line, and we alternate at this.) I love to plot our course on the chart, and though my pencil lines are not quite as neat as Mother's were, Papa says I am doing very well.

"You can't imagine what a comfort it is," said Papa, "to know that you and Mother could manage this ship on your own, if anything happened to me."

"Nothing's going to happen to you, Papa!" I cried out.

He smiled. "No need to worry, but even so, I like knowing that if unlikely circumstances arose, the ship would be in good hands."

"And the mates?"

"I'll speak plainly, Celia, for you are old enough to hear this. Mr. Grimes, though as able as any, I would not trust to have our interest at heart."

"And Isaac and Nate?"

"I trust them both completely, and Isaac could run the ship, with Nate's help, but you are the better navigator, and Nate does not yet know navigation. You, my dear, have a special knack for it."

"I like it, Papa. It's better than learning anything else. What good is the Latin, which Mother is making me learn?"

"It may come in useful, too, some day."

"I would be better off learning some native tongue, for I think it most unlikely that we would arrive at some foreign shore and find the savages speaking Latin."

Papa laughed. "Mother's father taught her Latin. You know he was a minister, a very learned man, and liked, in his old age, to have his daughter read to him. It gives her pleasure to keep it up, to pass it on to you. It's a small thing, Celia, to do to make her happy, and besides, it keeps your mind nimble."

Nimble indeed. You can imagine, though, how pleased I was with Papa's praise. I'd like to be a captain's wife when I grow up (it is no secret to you, dear Abigail, whom I would wish that captain to be), and I could help him run the ship, he wouldn't need his mates at all.

But now I'll say something that will shock you even more. Sometimes I think I should like to be a captain myself. Can you imagine what it would be like for a woman to be a captain?

Mother says it's nearly time for me to put my pen away and go to bed. And here I haven't even told you the news that I started out to write! We went through such a storm last night. A blizzard, with icy winds and sleet, and then, would you believe it, snow! This morning it finally stopped, and though the seas were still rough I was able to go up on deck. Mother wanted me to stay below, but Toby needs his exercise, and finally Mother had to admit that having him cooped up all day below would not be good for anyone's temper. There was snow everywhere. How strange the ship looked, as if it had all been painted white. It felt as if we were on real land, except for the fact that it never would stay level. Because the sky was grey and the sea was grey, I could imagine that all around us, far in the distance, were more fields of snow.

Toby was very excited and ran around in circles. Nate threw a snowball for him and he chased it, but could not find it in the fallen snow, though he dug frantically and his muzzle looked like he had a white beard. I threw a snowball at Nate, and he laughed and asked, "Is that a declaration of war?"

"It is!" I cried, and ducked behind the trypots, before he could get his snowball made. We had such great fun, with Toby running back and forth between us and barking all the time.

I had to quit when my hands got so cold I could no longer feel my fingers. I called a truce. Nate took my hands in his, peeled off my gloves, and blew on my frozen fingers to make them warm. Oh, Abigail, I would gladly let my fingers freeze every day if he would bring them up close to his lips and blow on them with his wonderful, warm breath!

"I think it's time for you to go down and have Mr. Prater bring you some hot tea," said Nate.

"Will you come, too?" I asked him.

"Not now," said Nate, and he grinned. "Some of us have work to do on this ship."

"Oh," I said, "if that's the case!" And I sounded as haughty as I could, but I could not muster it for long because Nate winked at me. I turned and waved to him at the top of the companionway, and he had been watching me, and waved back.

Mother, as can be expected, scolded me for staying out so long, for getting myself so cold, for getting my hems so wet. But I didn't mind one bit, I felt so happy.

But now I really must bring this letter to a close, for even Papa has been reminding me of the hour.

So, good night, dear Abigail.

Love from your happy cousin,
Celia

June 26, 1857

My Dear Abigail,

If only you were here! You would be such a comfort, for you would know what I am feeling now. But you are on the other side of the world and I have nothing but this thin piece of paper, this slender pen, and they must take your place.

I cannot sleep, though Mother has sent me to my cabin and ordered me to. I have come to my cabin, though I want to be with Papa up on deck, but sleep I won't. I won't sleep until Nate's whaleboat is found and he is safely back on board. Mother can confine me to my cabin, but she cannot make me sleep. I won't speak to her even if she comes knocking on my cabin door and in fact I may never speak to her again.

This morning began fair enough—the sun was shining, the water smooth. There was no hint of what was coming, no hint of any trouble lying in wait. Yet on a whaling voyage trouble is always lurking; I must never forget that. We live day by day, hour by hour. It can be perfect serenity one moment, then catastrophe the next. The men are always joyful to hear the sound "There blows!" (for nothing is worse than weeks and weeks without sight of a whale), yet every time I hear that cry I feel as if a piece of ice was rubbed along my spine. Every time the boats go out I can't think about anything else until they are safely back.

This morning I was awakened early by the cry "There blows!" A bowhead whale was raised and Papa ordered all four boats lowered and they went in chase. Nate's boat, the waistboat, was closest, and the boat-steerer threw his harpoon and made fast. He and Nate changed places in the boat—a tricky job. (It is the mate who kills the whale with his lance once the whale is tired out.) They had a long, wild ride, but then the whale sounded and did not come up again and they had to cut their rope. And then no sight of whales at all, so eventually Papa called all the boats back. (I know all the signals now and can run the flags up the mast myself.)

At dinner Nate was feeling very low. "We almost had her," he kept saying. Mr. Grimes seemed to enjoy Nate's failure—he's such a hateful man!—and commented that when Nate has a bit more experience he'll know how to deal the death blow to such a whale before he sounds. Nate bit into his hardtack with such force I thought he'd crack his tooth, but he didn't say anything in return.

After dinner the cry again, "There blows!" Two bowheads spotted this time, and all the boats were lowered once again, though Papa was concerned because the weather was changing fast. The sun was hidden behind thick clouds and fog was moving in.

Nate's boat was the first one off. "I'll bring one back this time," he promised me. And I was happy to see the boat go off, and waved from the deck, imagining Nate coming back with a huge whale in tow, and Mr. Grimes, with all his "expariance" (as he pronounces it) coming back with none.

Mr. Grimes's boat came back first, but without a whale. (I confess that I was glad, because as much as I want us to get all the whales we can, I hate to give Mr. Grimes any satisfaction.) He reported that the other boats were following behind. The starboard boat (under the command of Ephraim Millard, who is well respected by Papa) came back after a while, but he reported, contrary to Mr. Grimes, that Nate's boat had gone in pursuit of a whale and he thought that Isaac's boat had gone along. He said the fog was worse and it was hard to see very far, and so Papa ordered the ringing of the ship's bell.

An hour or so later Isaac's boat came back. What suspense I was in all that time! He said he'd lost sight of the whale and of Nate's boat. He reported that the fog was getting thicker and if it weren't for the sound of the bell, he may not have found his way back to the ship at all. You can imagine how I felt then, knowing that Nate was most likely even farther off, maybe too far to even hear the bell! And surely Mr. Grimes was at fault for not giving an accurate account of the danger of the fog and for not suggesting the ringing of the bell. (I think he lied about the other boats following back behind him because he did not want Papa to know that he was aware he was the only one to give up the chase.)

Isaac and Ephraim volunteered to go in search of the missing boat, and the starboard boat was lowered again. Their lantern was soon out of sight in the fog, but I could hear them firing off a gun. At length they came back, much dejected. Mr. Grimes said that was what happened when you put a boy in command of a whaleboat—though not so that Papa could hear him— but Ephraim defended Nate and said he was as able a seaman as any.

Then, Abigail, evening came and the ship was surrounded by darkness. No moon, no stars, the sea and sky just black nothing. Somewhere, Nate's little boat was bobbing in the waves. They've put lanterns up in the rigging. Papa reassured me that it is not uncommon for a whaleboat to get too far from the ship to make it back at night and that there was food and water for several days on board. I know from the chart that we are nowhere near land of any kind. If Nate is lost at sea he'll drift forever!

At supper Mr. Grimes said Nate should have seen the fog coming on and not put his men at risk, and Mother agreed with him! When we were alone in the cabin (Mother going calmly about the business of sewing as if nothing were amiss!) I told her that it was cruel of her to side with Mr. Grimes and criticize Nate when all he was doing was trying to bring a whale back for us (and I know he wouldn't have tried so hard if Mr. Grimes hadn't blamed him for not catching the one he lost this morning).

"He's young, and sometimes his judgement is not the best," is what Mother said. Can you imagine her saying that! With Nate out there in the dark, and for all we knew maybe miles and miles away and maybe even—dear Lord, it frightens me to even write it here—maybe even injured or killed by the whale he was pursuing!

"You don't care if Nate is lost or found! You don't care if he's alive or dead!" I cried.

"Of course I care," Mother said.

"You don't care!" I said. "You hate him and just like Mr. Grimes you wish to be rid of him. And don't think I don't know why!"

Mother took in a deep breath and did not respond to what I said. Instead she said, in that false, calm voice she uses when she's struggled with herself to keep control and won (the voice that makes me want to scream), "I won't have you speaking to me this way. It is time for you to go to your cabin and go to sleep."

"I'll go to my cabin gladly," I said. And slammed the door behind me so fast my skirt got caught and I had to open it and close it once again.

It felt almost good, at first, to be that angry, for while I was angry at Mother I was distracted from my fear about Nate. I've discovered that I can accommodate only one strong emotion at a time. When my anger had subsided, then my fear took over, and how much worse that was! I thought of Nate when I'd last seen him, calling out "I'll bring one back," and wished I had cried out, "I don't care about the whale, it's you I want you to bring back." And I lay on my bunk and wept into my pillow until I had no tears left in me at all.

There is no one in the world except you, dear Abigail, who knows how I feel. No one else who can imagine what this waiting is like for me. Papa is worried for Nate, I know. (I peeked up on deck, and he has not come down, though Mother is asleep in their cabin. He's had the men burn a fire in the trypots so that a light can be seen on the ship, though it is foggy still.)

Pray for me, Abigail, pray for Nate! (I know you won't be reading this letter for months, yet somehow, as I write, I feel that you can hear me.) I prayed myself, but found no comfort in it. Like Papa, I don't believe you can rely on prayers, in fact, I no longer trust that mine will be listened to. But if you pray, Abigail, your prayers will be answered I know, for you have always had such faith, such certainty.

The ship is barely rocking now. It is as if the fog has flattened all the waves, like a vast pillow on the sea. How quiet it is, except for the ringing now and then of the ship's bell. Nate, please hear it. Nate, please come back!

There, I have covered both sides of two sheets. I am all written out. I will try to sleep now. I will hug Toby close and try to fall asleep quickly without letting my mind dwell on anything at all. And when I wake up it will be morning and maybe Nate's boat will be back—please, Lord!—and he and his crew all safe again.

—Celia

June 27, 1857

Dearest Abigail,

A whole day has passed, and now it is night again.

I woke up this morning full of hope, but one glance at Papa's face and I knew the worst. The fog lifted somewhat in the early afternoon, and Papa ordered all the whaleboats out to comb the sea. He went too, leaving Mother and me in charge of the ship, with only Mr. Prater and the cook. It was my job to ring the bell every quarter of an hour, and I was glad of something more to do than scan the sea with the spyglass, looking, looking, and seeing nothing at all. I stood up in the bow and cried out Nate's name into the whiteness.

Mother was to shoot off the gun (one of many things that I am surprised she can do) if they should return to the ship, if there was any news. I had been resolved to not talk to her today, but it is strange, I no longer feel angry at her as I had been. I am too worried to be angry, and I know that she is worried, too. Before Papa left she hugged him and I heard her say "Be careful, Daniel; we can't lose you, too."

"I'll be careful," Papa promised her. She set her face to be brave. I had been thinking only of Nate, of rescuing him, so you can imagine how it added to my worry that Papa was out there also, and how I felt when I saw that the fog was getting worse.

Mr. Grimes's boat was the first one back, and I was sure he hadn't risked much in the looking. Papa's boat was later. He told Mother that the fog was so thick that when he was a short distance off, it not only hid the ship but it muffled the sound of the bell. He was anxious about Isaac, I could tell, though he did not say so. I realized they had been searching not only for Nate's boat, but for any pieces of it. I had not thought of the possibility that the boat could have been stove by a whale, that Nate could have been injured, or thrown into the sea. Such cold water! No one could last very long in this sea!

Dear Abigail, he must be safe somewhere in this sea, just lost, but safe, don't you think so? If he were dead I would know it, wouldn't I?

At last Isaac returned. They had spotted something promising and rowed to it, but it proved not to be a boat but the carcass of a pilot whale, not worth bringing back. It was a somber dinner. I could not eat a thing and I did not want to talk to anyone. Mr. Prater muttered that he feared something like this would happen, "us having set sail on a Friday." I had thought having Sallie die and Joseph Sylva drowned was bad luck enough, but Mr. Prater seems to expect even more.

"Hush now, Mr. Prater," Papa said. "There's nothing in that superstition."

"Aye, but there is. That young mate, such a fine young lad, he's lost for sure, and all because he wanted so much to please you with a whale."

"He was a fool, that's what he was," said Mr. Grimes. "And it's not just him that's lost but all his crew, and he's the one to blame. We've wasted time enough on this futile search. It's time we sailed on and went about our business."

"Until those men are found, or some remnant of their boat, that is our only business, Mr. Grimes," said Papa, "as long as I am master of this ship."

Mr. Grimes got up from the table and exited the room, not before giving a small nod in Mother's direction. "Excuse me, Madam," he said.

It was all silent after he left. Mr. Prater went about the clearing of the table, shaking his head mournfully all the while. We went back to our cabin and Mother asked if I would like to play backgammon—we got a fine set in the Sandwich Islands—but I did not have the heart for it, though it was sweet of her to want to cheer me up, for I could tell she did not have the heart for it either, but just wanted to go to bed, for she was as tired as I.

"Do you think they're still alive?" I asked her.

"Papa thinks so," she said. "I have been praying for them. That is the best that we can do." She looked up at me. "Would you like us to pray together?"

I did not feel like praying any more than I felt like playing backgammon. But I nodded and Mother came and sat beside me. She took my hand and bowed her head. And so we prayed together. It did not ease my heart to pray, and yet it was of some comfort having Mother close beside me.

The bell keeps ringing. It will ring all night. Papa will not give up.

I am so tired, everything in me hurts. And yet I cannot think of me, I can think only of Nate.

Do you think this is what love is then, Abigail, the way I feel for Nate?

—Celia

June 28, 1857

Dearest Abigail,

I finally fell asleep, but it was nearly morning when I did so. When I awoke I could see nothing but fog out of my little porthole—the sea and sky were one. No news of Nate. At breakfast no one spoke much except for Mr. Prater, who got on everybody's nerves by muttering, "A sorry thing, a sorry thing," until Papa said, "Come now, Mr. Prater, enough of that. The fog will lift and we'll find our men."

Toby was restless all day, yapping at the slightest provocation. He made me feel like slapping him, which, dear Abigail, I confess I actually resorted to. I felt so terrible afterwards, for he gave a little whimper and looked up at me with such a look, and then I took him in my arms and cried and cried. The ringing of the bell drove me nearly crazy, too.

The fog was so thick that we almost hit another ship, the *Tidemarsh*, out of Mattapoisett. We found ourselves right close to them, so suddenly, without warning. They appeared like a ghost ship out of the fog. Papa told the captain about our lost boat. They had seen no sign of it, but said they would watch for it and pass the word to other ships. Papa and Captain Fredericks exchanged other news, but I found I had no interest in such things anymore. Nor in the oranges Captain Fredericks bestowed on us.

By afternoon the fog began to clear and the whaleboats went out, two at a time. If they had all gone out then Mother and I would have been employed taking care of the ship, but as there was now enough crew left on board, we had nothing to do but sew, which is quite worse than doing nothing. As soon as it was dark Papa had a fire going in the tryworks.

"A waste, I tell you," said Mr. Grimes. "That boat is gone for good."

Papa would not even answer him.

Mother again offered to play backgammon with me and so we did, though how could I care about moving little markers around a board?

"Do you think it will be clear again tomorrow?" I asked.

"I hope it will. The Bering Sea is often very foggy. The last time I was here I remember fog for days and days."

"But since it was clear today, and still is clear tonight, we won't have fog tomorrow, surely."

"It could be clear one day and fog come in the next," said Mother.

"But if it's clear, then we'll find them, won't we?"

"Celia—" Mother began, and she tilted her head as she looked at me, as if that would soften what she was about to say. "It is possible that the boat was stove. It's possible that they did not survive. And even if they survived their encounter with the whale, they may have traveled too far in the wrong direction for—"

"No!" I cried. "Don't say that!"

"Celia," said Mother. "Some things have to be said."

"Why did you give up on them? Papa hasn't given up on them!"

"I haven't given up on them, Celia. I have been

praying for them. But I just want you to accept what may be true, the possibility—"

"No!" I said. "I can't!"

"It's late, Celia. It's time you went to bed now," said Mother.

And so I have come to my cabin, not to go to bed, but to write to you. But I cannot bear to stay below any longer, and Papa, I know, is still up on deck. I shall join him there later, if I can.

—C.

added later

I am too exhausted to write, but I must write to you. And I shall write about it exactly as it happened.

Mother was in her cabin and I sneaked up the companionway. It was cold on deck, but warmer near the trypots' blaze. Papa was leaning on the rails looking out at the sea. I ducked under his arm and snuggled against him.

"This is a surprise," he said, and he kissed my head. "Does Mother know you're up here?"

"Not exactly, but—"

"Oh, I see," he said.

"It's because—"

"Shh," he said. He pointed at the sky. "Look, Celia, the stars are out."

I looked up at the sky and there were the stars, like old friends. They hadn't been erased by all the fog, but had been there waiting patiently behind it all along.

"There's a compass in every whaleboat, isn't there?" I said.

"Yes," said Papa.

"How long can the provisions last?"

"If they're careful, many days."

"They'll be cold, won't they?"

"Yes, but they're tough men," he said, and he hugged me close against his side.

And it was then, as I was watching the sea, that I saw a flicker far in the distance. "What's that light, Papa?" I asked.

He hadn't noticed it. "Must be a whaler who's had better luck than us, boiling."

"But it's odd the way it comes and goes," I said. I pointed. "Look."

He saw it finally. "It is odd," he said. "Must be the waves. But then it must be something smaller, closer by—dear God," he cried, and he gripped my shoulder, "let it be so!"

All hands were called on deck and all four whale-boats with lanterns lowered. Mother came rushing up on deck. When she saw me, she took her shawl off and wrapped it over my shoulders. Mr. Prater was in a flurry, but Mother ordered him to bring blankets up on deck and to tell the cook to heat up food and drink.

"In case it be our men, or any men out lost on this cold night," she said.

I watched the whaleboats heading out, the lanterns flickering off in the distance. I could see three lights, then four, then two, then four again. How long it took! I think I held my breath, but of course I could not have held it all that time.

It was them, Abigail, it was them! And Nate was safe, and Nate was back! Oh, dear Abigail, I've wanted nothing else. I cannot write another drop. Adieu for now.

Your most affectionate cousin,
Celia

June 29, 1857

Dear, dear Abigail,

Oh, what a celebration we had! We had a feast of roast chicken (not Miriam, I promise you) and dumplings and apple fritters and pie. We had music and dancing and everybody (Mr. Grimes excepted) danced and Toby, too (I held his paws). Papa gave grog to all the crew.

Not only is Nate back, but the carcass of the bowhead whale that he slew was found as well. (They had been too exhausted to tow it all the way to the *Jupiter* and had cut it loose.) There was not as much of the whale as there would have been two days ago and the smell, dear Abigail, the smell was something even the men complained about, and judging from the smells they produce themselves and never notice, that should tell you quite a lot. But still we got enough barrels of oil to make Nate proud and to make Mr. Grimes keep his comments to himself, for once.

When Nate's whaleboat got back to us, I was so happy to see his face I forgot all my decorum. I cried, "Nate!" and when he made it up on the deck I flung my arms around him. He was so weak I nearly knocked him off his balance.

"Well, this is quite a welcome," he said, and everybody laughed. You can imagine how mortified I was.

Then Papa said, "It was Celia who first spotted your light, and made me realize what it was."

Then do you know what Nate did, Abigail? He took my hand and kissed it! Oh, Abigail, I can say nothing more! And so I will end here, because I don't think I could ever be happier than I am tonight.

Your most happy cousin,
Celia

July 11, 1857

Dearest Abigail,

And now it's been just as it was before. No whales, day after day, and everyone impatient once again. All we caught this whole week was a walrus, the ugliest creature I have ever seen.

One crewman from Nate's boat has lost two fingers to frostbite, another has a cough so bad it shakes the ship. My throat has been sore for several days and anything but tea is hard to swallow.

Your cousin,
Celia

July 20, 1857

Dearest Abigail,

We made it through the Unimak Passage and now are in Bristol Bay, the farthest north I've ever been. There are whaleships all around us. You can see a dozen at a time! It is just like a colony here, and very gay, with lots of gamming. I was hoping the Winslows would come, but they have not. Will I ever see them again?

We have twice gammed with the *Devonshire*. It was Captain Strickley whom we met early in our voyage, who gave us the three hens, one of them my Miriam.

He was most amazed to see her and says he will write to his children about her. One of his little daughters was very ill when he last received a letter from home and he has been most anxious for news.

All these days since I last wrote we've caught only two bowheads, one so small it didn't give much oil. Papa says there are more whaling ships than whales these days, and no one is catching many whales. Everyone watches to see who is boiling, who was lucky the day before. I am sure the whales are smart enough to see this fleet of ships and take themselves far off.

Some natives came aboard our ship and were very interested in staring at Mother and me. They were most curious about Toby. He could not make them out, and kept racing in circles around them and sniffing and yapping at their fur-trimmed boots. We had begun boiling the day they visited and they were eager to have some scraps of blubber—can you imagine, they eat it raw! (The very smell of it would make you ill.)

Papa got me a coat with a great fur collar (in trade for some tobacco). Now I look like a wild creature myself, and Toby yaps whenever I put it on.

"If he keeps that up, I'll see him as a coat one day soon," said Mr. Grimes.

I have gotten some carvings of seals from them, for you and for Willie and the boys. (Each is so smoothly polished you'll want to rub your cheek along it.) Papa bought a coat for Willie, too. I hope we will be home soon enough so it will fit him. (I can imagine how much he's grown!) But how that will be if we don't get more whales soon, I do not know.

Your loving cousin,
Celia

July 26, 1857

Dearest Abigail,

I've made a new friend! Her name is Phoebe Nickerson and her family's from Provincetown. She has an older sister, Lydia, who is, in Mother's words "most stately," and an older brother, Barnabas, who is before the mast. She has been on two whaling cruises. (Her father is one eighth owner of their bark, the *Orion* out of New Bedford.)

We liked each other immediately. When Mother told her mother about this lovely girl our age in Honolulu, Jerusha Doane, I caught Phoebe covering her smile with her hand. It turns out she knows Jerusha, too, and her opinion of her is exactly my own, though her mother (and her sister, too) find Jerusha a charming young lady.

Phoebe is very fortunate to have a sister for company (though she would be more fortunate still if Lydia had not quite so serious a disposition). I overheard Mother saying to Papa that it was a pity the younger sister was "so plain," but in truth, I think that Phoebe's happy demeanor makes her by far the fairer sister of the two.

We shall gam with them again tomorrow!

Your most affectionate cousin,

Celia

P.S. Phoebe has a cat who's recently had kittens. I am hoping Papa will let me have one, if she offers one to me (I think she might). I loved best the white one with the black eyepatch and black-tipped tail.

July 29, 1857

Dear Abigail,

Yesterday I heard Nate ask Isaac if he didn't think Lydia a "great beauty."

"That she is," Isaac answered, "but I'm spoken for."

"Fortunately, I'm not," said Nate.

What does this mean?

—Celia

P.S. Lydia does have shiny black curls and the bluest eyes you've ever seen, but her neck is far too long.

July 31, 1857

Dear Abigail,

We gammed with the Nickersons today, and I would have been so happy, except that Nate leaped at the chance to row us over, and although Phoebe and I were busy together I could see that he seized every opportunity to be near Lydia.

What am I going to do?

—Celia

P.S. Her teeth protrude most noticeably in profile.

August 2, 1857

Dearest Abigail,

We are leaving these whaling grounds soon—Papa says there are no whales left here (and indeed we'll never fill our barrels and never get home if something doesn't change) and we are going to sail through the Bering Strait to try our luck farther north. Mother is

· 135 ·

worried because it's late in the season and she is afraid of the ice, but she trusts Papa's decision.

The Nickersons won't be coming (they'll be heading south) and, dear Abigail, I am very sad on all accounts but one.

I overheard Mother telling Papa tonight that she believed Nate was "smitten with Lydia."

"No wonder," Papa said. "She's a fine-looking young lady."

Oh, Abigail!

I asked Phoebe what she thinks of Nate and she said she thought he was very nice. I asked her if Lydia thought so too and she said she believed she did. She says all the mates have been noticing Lydia, and her mother thinks it will be wiser to leave Lydia home on their next cruise, which is what Mother said as well. I wish they had left her home for this one.

Your cousin,
Celia

P.S. Phoebe has offered me a kitten, any one I want. She is the dearest girl in the world, excepting you.

August 4, 1857

Dearest Abigail,

Things couldn't be worse! The Nickersons are looking to replace their second mate (who was washed overboard in a storm near California), and Nate may leave us and take that place! Isaac said Nate is eager for advancement, but Mr. Prater said, "That young man would seek a place on that young lady's ship even if it were the cabin boy."

Nothing can make me happy now. Not even that sweet kitten.

Your miserable cousin,
Celia

August 7, 1857

Dearest Abigail,

We are heading North at last and Nate is with us still. Papa let Captain Nickerson know he was loath to part with his third mate, and Captain Nickerson is too good a friend of Papa's to lure away any of his crew.

Nate gave Lydia a scrimshaw corset busk, beautifully carved (Phoebe showed it to me), but Phoebe assured me they do not have an agreement.

Phoebe gave me the kitten when we said good-bye. It is very cute, but no consolation for my loss of her company. How lucky are girls who live on land and can have their friends near them day after day, week after week, year after year. Here you make such close friends (I think so often of the Winslows) and then you don't know when you shall see them again. If ever. (I cannot bear to think of that!)

I gave her a drawing she liked of Toby asleep in the waistboat. (The only time when he is still enough for me to draw him is when he is asleep.) She is very fond of Toby and I wish I had a puppy to give to her. She thinks I have talent as an artist, which is most kind of her.

I spoke to Nate on deck yesterday, and he asked me if I wasn't sad to be sailing north and leaving my good friends behind.

"I would be far sadder staying behind where there are no whales," I said. "Since it's whales we need, not friends."

"Well!" said Nate, "now that's a harsh reply I wouldn't have expected from you, Celia."

Oh, he is so obtuse, Abigail! Does he really have no idea of how I suffered when he was under the spell of the "fair" Lydia? "Probably not," I hear you say, and you are most likely right. He likes me well enough, but sees me as a child, nothing more.

What can I do, Abigail, to make him see me for what I am?

Your cousin,
Celia

P.S. I was going to name the kitten Cleopawtra (which I thought a clever pun), but when I tried to call her by it, it seemed so big a name, I've named her Fluff, instead. Toby, as you would have predicted, is overcome by jealousy. Miriam treats her like another chicken.

August 13, 1857

Dear Abigail,

Fluff is doing poorly. Mother thinks she may have been weaned too early. She doesn't eat and barely drinks. I have tried everything, but nothing helps. I wonder how Phoebe's other kittens are faring.

I wonder how Phoebe is.

Nate has said nothing more about Lydia. I hope he has forgotten about her by now. He was writing a letter the other evening and had to lay it aside when he was called on deck. I did not really read it, but just took a tiny peek, and was reassured to see he was writing to his family, not to HER.

There is nothing much for me to write. All there is here is ice. Ice and more ice. Isaac says if a man fell overboard he wouldn't last a minute in the water, it is so cold. They have raised a number of bowheads but can't get close to one. No one can stay in the lookout for very long.

Mother has been most annoying. She has taken up tatting (Phoebe's mother started her and gave her a quantity of thread) and wants me to do it, too, but I refuse. I would rather twiddle my thumbs.

—Celia

August 15, 1857

Dearest Abigail,

Fluff is dead.

I knew that she was going to die. I knew it for days, yet that did not make it any easier.

Dying moves along and changes, bit by bit, but death is simply just death.

Mother gave me some muslin to wrap Fluff in, and the carpenter made a little box for her. Papa read some words of Scripture and we committed her body to the deep, which is the fancy way of saying I threw the box overboard.

At least Sallie was buried in real ground in a green churchyard.

I hate this place. I wish that I were home.

I am sorry if this letter sounds so gloomy, but I have nothing to report that isn't gloomy.

—Celia

September 11, 1857

Dearest Abigail,

Ice, ice, and more ice! There is not much to write to you about these past weeks. All this time in the Arctic Ocean and we've gotten only one bowhead. There are lots of them, but they are hard to catch. They dive under ice floes and the whaleboats cannot follow them.

We are heading south again soon. Papa and Mr. Grimes argued about it. Mr. Grimes says there are a lot of bowheads to be had and we shouldn't leave yet. Papa is concerned about being frozen in. Mother thinks we have already stayed too long and is afraid we could be trapped up here. Mr. Grimes said Papa should stop listening to a woman's fears. Papa said he was listening to his own judgement.

I am tired of everything and have nothing more to write. I am sorry that I have turned out to be such a lugubrious correspondent. I won't write again until I have something cheerful, or at least something interesting to say!

—Celia

September 20, 1857

Dearest Abigail,

I have something to write to you about at last, but how I wish I didn't! I would prefer the dullest, nothing-to-write-about days to what happened yesterday.

We made it through the Bering Strait, and I felt so relieved (and Mother, too) that we were leaving the Arctic in time. I'd thought once we had escaped the risk of being frozen in, we'd left all danger behind. I'd forgotten what whaling's like: You are safe only for the moment you are in; there's no promise of safety in the next.

A week later we got another bowhead, which made us all happy, me especially, since it gave 175 barrels of oil and brings us that much closer to getting home. Papa decided to stay in this area a little longer, then maybe try the Kodiak Grounds, which was such a disappointment, for I had fixed my mind on the Sandwich Islands. I was picturing those green hills—I was dreaming of green!—and I was thinking about letters from you waiting for me there, and thinking about friends I might see (not Jerusha, of course) and shops and town and the wonderful firm earth beneath my feet. I wished there would be something to make Papa change his mind and decide to head straight for the Sandwich Islands right away. Now hear what I brought upon us by my wishing!

In the middle of the night there was such a terrible jolt I was thrown off my bunk and the whole ship trembled. A minute later, Mother flung open my door.

"Get dressed quickly," she said. "Wear your warmest clothes." I could hear running and shouting all over the ship. Outside my porthole, all was dark. Mother came bursting back and helped me dress.

"What's happened?" I cried.

"We've struck a cake of ice," she said. "The ship has sprung a leak. We need to be on deck."

"Oh, Mother!" I cried.

She hugged me quickly. "We'll be all right, Celie,"

· 143 ·

she said, calling me by my baby name. "If we need to leave the ship we have our sturdy whaleboats, and the seas are not too high."

Abandon ship?!

I pulled on the boots she handed me and followed her up the companionway, Toby in my arms.

All hands were racing about, with Papa in the center of the deck, and Mr. Grimes barking out orders to the crew. Nate went dashing by me without even giving me a smile. Mother hurried me over to the starboard boat. Mr. Prater was ready to assist me in, but I thrust Toby at him and climbed in myself, and he handed Toby up to me. Mother dropped a pile of blankets beside me.

"I need to help Papa," she said. "Wait here with Toby." And she was gone. Toby was yipping and scrambling in my arms. I wanted to be on deck, too, helping out, not stuck waiting and watching, but I waited, and I rubbed Toby to try to calm him down. Suddenly I remembered Miriam and all the other animals.

I set Toby on the floor of the boat. "Stay here!" I told him in as fierce a voice I could. I grabbed a blanket and jumped out of the boat and ran to Miriam's cage in steerage below. I knew there was no way I could wrestle her cage up on deck, so I took her out and wrapped her in the blanket. She was too alarmed to squawk.

I ran into Isaac on the companionway. "Celia, what are you doing here?" he asked.

I folded back a corner of the blanket so he could see Miriam's head. "Will you get Ophelia and the other animals?" I asked.

"I'm not sure that will be necessary," said Isaac. "We're not giving up the ship yet."

"But if we do, you'll rescue them, won't you?" I waited for a second. "Please?"

"I'll do what I can," Isaac said.

Toby was overjoyed by my return, but less overjoyed to have Miriam there, too. We huddled together, for it was a cold night. I thought maybe Mother had forgotten me there in the whaleboat, but finally, after a long time, she returned.

"We can go back to our cabins now," she said. "The damage was less than Papa first thought and the repair is holding." I handed Toby out to her and climbed out of the boat. Then Mother noticed the bundle in my arms and asked me what it was. I let Miriam peek out.

"You weren't to leave that whaleboat," she said to me.

"I couldn't leave Miriam behind."

"Put her back in her cage and go to your cabin. When there is an emergency on board this ship, Celia, you do exactly as you're told, and you don't go below after chickens."

"You don't understand, Mother, it's not chickens, it's Miriam!"

"What I understand is that I told you to stay in the whaleboat and you disobeyed."

"You don't understand anything!" I cried.

Papa spoke to me that night in the sternest voice he's ever used to me. "Celia," he began, "I am distressed to hear that you didn't follow orders. If we had to abandon ship quickly you could have been caught below."

"But I couldn't just leave Miriam behind."

"On a ship, Celia, you do exactly as you're told, no matter what you're feeling," Papa said. "Your life, all our lives, may depend on it."

"Oh, Papa," I said, and I leaned against his chest and cried.

"It's all over. We're safe now," he said, and he stroked my head.

And so we are heading straight to the Sandwich Islands with crew manning the pump the whole time. And soon—barring any new disasters—we shall be in Honolulu and I shall post you all my recent letters.

(I sent two with a merchant ship several weeks ago.)

You would have gone back for Miriam, wouldn't you?

—Celia

October 19, 1857

Dear Abigail,

Such a feast of letters! And yet so sad to hear you all rejoice in Sallie's birth. Surely you must now know about our sorrow. Mother cried when she read the letter from Grandmother. How hard it is to be so far away that letters are a life behind.

We went first thing to visit Sallie's grave. Mrs. Farnsworth has kept it very nicely. Mother says she doesn't want to stay here very long—everything about the Sandwich Islands makes her melancholy—and we shall leave as soon as repairs are done to the ship. But how wonderful to be on land again and everything even more green than I had remembered it.

I was hoping I might see the Winslows or Phoebe, but so far we have no news of them. Tomorrow I have no choice but to visit with the Doanes. We have only just arrived, but Mrs. Doane discovered it immediately. She discovers everything.

If, as you wrote, your neighbor Martha Holbrook has a cousin Priscilla engaged to a Nathaniel Woodbridge who is at sea (a whaler or a merchant ship?), it may not be the same Nathaniel Woodbridge, for I am certain he is not the only one from Brewster to bear that name. Find out all you can! And I shall try the name Priscilla on him and see if it has any effect.

I must hurry this into the post, for Mother wants the family to know we arrived back here safely and she hasn't had time to write yet herself. Tell Willie we were delighted with his letter and we miss him very much. I am glad he is happy, but hope he won't forget us entirely.

Love to you and all our dear family,
your cousin Celia

October 20, 1857

Dear Abigail,

It is late at night but I had to write to you. I've heard such terrible news today: the Winslows are lost at sea!

I hate Mrs. Doane. I hate Jerusha.

We had tea with them this afternoon, and Mother asked if they knew when the Winslows left Honolulu and Mrs. Doane leaned forward in her chair and exclaimed, "But surely you've heard!"

"Heard what?" Mother asked.

"The tragedy," said Mrs. Doane, and she seemed almost gleeful to have such exciting news to impart. "Their ship was wrecked off Mozambique and everyone was lost."

"Oh, dear God," Mother cried. "Can this be true?"

Mrs. Doane said that although it had not been reported in the papers yet, she'd had it on excellent authority, her husband's former mate, now captain of a schooner out of Salem.

"When he told me," she said, "not knowing they were dear friends of mine, that the bark *Ranger* had been wrecked in a typhoon, you can imagine how shocked I was. I nearly fainted. I told Mary Winslow that they should never take young children like that with them on their cruise, but did they listen to me?"

I could not bear to hear another word. I sprang up from my chair. "I'm going back," I said.

"Are you feeling all right, dear?" asked Mrs. Doane. "Would you like Jerusha to accompany you?"

I shook my head and bolted from the room. I ran all the way back to our rooms. Thank goodness Papa had just returned himself and I was able to tell him what had happened. He hugged me close and I could feel his chest heaving, although he did not cry out loud.

When Mother returned she was angry at me for running off the way I did. Papa said he thought under the circumstances I should be excused.

"There is never an excuse for rudeness," Mother said.

"Oh, Ann," he said, and he put his hand on her shoulder.

She moaned. "My poor, dear Mary! Those poor children!" Then she sank right down and wept.

I can't believe they are all dead. This evening Papa spoke with some acquaintances who confirmed Mrs. Doane's rumor about the bark *Ranger*. I asked him if it might be a different vessel since the Winslow's whaler was rigged as a ship, not a bark, but he said I should not take hope in that.

"And Mozambique. Would they have gone that way?" I asked.

"I recall Captain Winslow once mentioning the grounds in Delgado Bay," said Papa, "though I had not expected them to head there."

Oh Abigail! I keep picturing Content and Robin. I remember how they clung to me when we left, their warm little bodies against mine. That they should be drowned in the sea!

This is unbearable. All of it.

—Celia

November 3, 1857

Dear Abigail,

I am sorry I have not written you for a while, but I have not felt like writing for many days. In truth I have not felt like doing much of anything. But we will be leaving Honolulu on Thursday and I wanted to be sure to get a letter posted to you.

I will be glad to leave this place. Everywhere I go I am reminded of the Winslows, and although I know it cannot be, there's part of me that keeps expecting to see them here. The clergyman's wife, Mrs. Prollock, organized a picnic trip, but I did not go, though Mother insisted it would do me good. Nor did I go riding with Mrs. Farnsworth and some friends of hers. The last time I was on horseback here was when the Winslows took me, the time that Captain Winslow flew off his horse, laughed, and climbed back on, and my dear little Content rode like a native.

It is difficult to be civil to the Doanes, who inflict

themselves upon us with regularity. I told Jerusha about meeting Phoebe, and she described her as the "homely sister," which made me want to smack her. She admitted that Lydia is "quite handsome," although she added it was "a pity about her teeth." I never thought I would feel an urge to defend anything about Lydia, especially her teeth, but Jerusha makes me want to contradict her, no matter what she says.

I was disappointed the Nickersons were not here. But I must confess that as much as I longed to see Phoebe I was a little relieved as well, for I am not eager for Nate to have his admiration of Lydia rekindled.

As for Martha's cousin, Priscilla, Isaac assures me that Nate has said nothing about being engaged to someone back home, though he admitted if Nate were engaged he is not sure Nate would own up to it because he "enjoys meeting young ladies." I asked Nate what he thought of the name Priscilla for our new goat. He said he had no opinion of it, so I pressed further and asked if he knew of any ladies by that name, and he claimed he could not remember any in particular. Either Priscilla is a love he chooses to keep secret, or a love totally forgotten. Or the two Nathaniels are not the same.

I have gotten no more letters from you since we

have been here, but I have read the three I did receive so many times the paper is nearly worn away. I thank you for your Christmas present, just received, of the little painting set. It is so precious! I did not feel like painting but I decided I should paint nevertheless, and so I have done several outdoor scenes to bring back to you. I wish I knew if you received the blue silk, but in case it never reached you I have bought you some other silk today—this is a deep indigo with a pattern, quite gorgeous! (though not as expensive as it looks). It should be enough for a dress as long as you don't plan on an enormous bustle.

Please don't tell Willie about the Winslows. I had written to him about Robin and Content and imagined how much they would enjoy each other's company, and he would be distressed to know their fate. Also, I think he would be more worried about our safe return. In truth, Abigail, I am worried too, and Mother is as well, though she does not speak of it.

I remember Captain Winslow telling us about the storm when their ship was dismasted. He laughed and said, "Our ship may fall apart, but we Winslows are indestructible."

Oh, would that it were so!

We are off now to the New Zealand Grounds. May

there be a dozen whales so we can fill our barrels quickly and return home at last. It has now been more than a year, one year and seventeen days to be exact, since we left New Bedford, more than a year since I have seen my home, and you and Willie and everyone I love. This cannot go on much longer.

I want to close my eyes and be in my sweet bed at home. I want this whole trip to disappear. Oh, Abigail, if only I hadn't come!

Your cousin,
Celia

November 27, 1857

Dearest Abigail,

I was seasick once again. This time, though, it took me only five days before I recovered, so I must be improving! In a hundred years or so I shall be a seasoned seaman and just hop back and forth from land to sea and never feel the difference.

We had some lovely weather for a week. I went fishing from the deck and did so well the cook served it up for dinner for all of us and even had some left for the fo'c'sle. Mr. Grimes was all set to enjoy his dinner until he found out its source, and then of course he had to complain of its taste.

We gammed with a French whaler yesterday. It was most amusing. Captain Duval knew little English and his pronunciation was so bad we had a regular game of charades to figure out what he was saying. Sperm whales he calls "cashalow." (Mother says its spelled "cachalot." The French use t's they don't bother to pronounce.) He had a beautiful parrot, which spoke only French, that he was eager to give to me. Papa would have let me take it, except Mother said no. She says I have pets enough.

Nate has been very cheerful and has not mentioned the Nickersons once. Poor Lydia, I think he has forgotten her. As for Martha's cousin Priscilla, if it is our Nate whom she is engaged to, I think she'd be advised to set her sights on another man. Priscilla the goat eats everything in sight. She would have eaten all of Mr. Prater's hat except he caught her in time so she had to satisfy herself with the brim.

When I look out at the sea it is so calm and blue and beautiful I can't believe it would hurt anyone. I keep feeling that the Winslows must be somewhere, safe. When I told Mother she said, "They are. They're in heaven, in God's care." But I don't mean that. I mean that I imagine them alive somewhere on this tranquil ocean, the *Ranger* with her sails all white against the sky.

How could God have let them die in such a horrible way?

—Celia

December 14, 1857

Dearest Abigail,

Such a scene in our cabin this morning! Mother heard noises in one of our trunks, and fearing it was rats (which she cannot stand) she asked me to investigate. It wasn't rats, it was cockroaches, the biggest you have ever seen, nearly as big as rats! Mr. Prater came running when he heard us screaming and went after them with a broom. They are so ferocious even Toby is afraid of them and Miriam won't eat them (although she considers the normal-sized variety a treat).

I haven't written for several weeks because there has not been much to write about. It has been quite hot and Papa has rigged a canopy on deck for us to sit under. We got a right whale last week, and I would rejoice except that it was a cow who had a little calf. The men killed the calf first, and the mother would not desert it and so was killed herself. I could not stand to watch.

The deck was such a greasy mess when they were done trying out, Papa had them wash it down with lime. And, oh, the stink! I needed to get used to it all over again.

We had a great rainshower this week and the crew stopped up all the scuppers and collected water on the deck. It was like one giant washtub, and everyone was doing laundry.

We gammed with another whaleship, the *Pegasus*, out of Stonington, Connecticut, and Captain Lawton said the sight of our petticoats drying on the line made him long for home. He had an ill-behaved Pug dog, who had no interest in being friends with Toby, although Toby tried his best.

Nate caught an albatross. Its wings outspread were wider than my arms. I did not like to see him teasing it, and so at last he let it go. It grieves me to admit that on a few, rare occasions Nate acts a bit like Willie. I wish he wouldn't give Mother reason to think him immature!

Captain Lawton said he'd heard a report of a disaster off the coast of Mozambique, but believed it was a whaleship out of New London. I was excited to hear this, for, as I pointed out, the Winslows' ship is out of Edgartown. Mother says I am wrong to hope. Why does she have to be like this?

Oh, Abigail, how I long for your company!

Your loving cousin,

Celia

December 25, 1857

Dearest Abigail,

Merry, merry Christmas!

My second Christmas on board this ship and I hope it is my last, for I so miss my Christmases at home. For our Christmas feast we had pineapples, which we got at an island where we stopped to cut wood, and plum tomatoes, and a roast wild pig. (I did not tell Ophelia.) I got a beautiful, tiny chest of drawers, inlaid with bone, for Rebecca's clothes, though I have her permission to share it with her, for it is perfect for storing small things. Papa and Mother bought it in Honolulu and have hidden it on board all this time.

The whole crew had gathered together for the singing of some carols, but we were interrupted by a cry of "There blows," and so the Christmas present for us all turned out to be a right whale, which is tied up now beside the ship. If only Santa Claus delivered whales directly to the ship to save the crew the work and danger of the hunt!

I hope Santa Claus was good to Willie (whether he's been good or not) and his stocking was stuffed full. Mother sent a trunkload of presents (the indigo silk for you included) before we left the Sandwich Islands, but I'm afraid you won't see them for a very long time.

Your most affectionate cousin,
Celia

January 7, 1858

Dearest Abigail,

Is it better to be a girl stuck aboard a whaler for months on end, as it travels from place to place, or to be a girl stuck on a small island forever?

Last week we stopped at one of the Cook Islands where there is a missionary family, the only white people living there. There are four daughters at home, ranging from Willie's age to mine. You can imagine how delighted they were to have us arrive, for their only society is the ships who stop there. The daughters were in raptures (I do not exaggerate when I use this word) to have a visit from another girl. The island is like a little paradise; you can pick lemons and limes right from the trees. We exchanged many gifts. The youngest daughter fell in love with Toby and cried when it was time for us to go. She would have been consoled, I'm sure, if I had decided to leave Toby behind. They waved the whole time we were rowed back to the ship and for all I know are waving, still.

I think it is better to be the girl on the whaler, except how I wish I had sisters for company and were not condemned to be alone with Mother.

Two of our crew are sick with a fever. Papa is very tired from caring for them.

Love from your ship-bound cousin,
Celia

January 15, 1858

Dearest Abigail,

I am so happy I can barely breathe! Such wonderful, wonderful news! The Winslows are alive! I felt all along that they must be, and now it is so!

I will try to be calm and let the story unfold for you as it happened, though I am so excited the news is ready to just tumble out.

Yesterday we spoke another ship, the *Cadmus* out of New Bedford, and the seas being too rough then we had to wait until today to gam. Captain Fisher is an old friend of Papa's and because the *Cadmus* was headed directly back to the Sandwich Islands he agreed to take our sick crewmen with them. We were invited to stay for dinner on the *Cadmus*. As we were finishing our soup, Papa was telling how sad we've been about the tragedy that struck dear friends of ours, the Winslows.

Captain Fisher dropped his spoon. "Tragedy!" he cried. "What happened?" For, it turned out, he knew them, too.

Mother put her hand upon his arm and said softly, "Their ship was wrecked in a typhoon off Mozambique, and all were lost."

"Mozambique?" asked Captain Fisher. "That must be wrong. For I saw them two weeks ago in the New Zealand Grounds."

"You saw them two weeks ago?" Papa asked. "But we learned about their deaths more than two months ago when we were in the Sandwich Islands."

"That's impossible," said Captain Fisher, "for we celebrated New Year's together on this ship and today is just the 15th of January."

I let out a cry, but Papa held up his hand.

"Wait," he said. "We must be sure of this. Are we both meaning Captain Henry Winslow of the *Ranger* out of Edgartown, his wife, Mary, and their two children, Robin and Content?"

"Yes," Captain Fisher said. "The very same."

"Then they're alive!" Mother cried.

"Oh, as alive as you or I," said Captain Fisher. "Why, the little girl was sitting in the same seat as Celia. And if you would like further proof, come into my cabin." And so we did and there he produced from his desk a little picture of a horse that Content had drawn for him, and there was the date on it as plain as we could see. Mrs. Doane's report had been all false.

Then what a grand time we had! Captain Fisher served grog to all his crew and Papa did the same with ours. I've never been so happy in my life!

Oh, Abigail, sometimes things do work out all right, don't they?

Your deliriously happy cousin,
Celia

January 23, 1858

My Dearest Abigail,

Papa has been ill with a fever and Mother is worried about him.

With Papa not there on deck, Mr. Grimes has been working the crew too hard and is most dictatorial. Papa was distressed to hear that when a crewman, Andrew

Crilly, complained they weren't being given enough food Mr. Grimes had him clapped in irons. Papa instructed Isaac to make inquiries of the cook and to free Andrew at once. Nate is doing his best to stay out of Mr. Grimes's way, for Mr. Grimes is eager to find fault and he will blame Nate whenever he can.

I hope Papa recovers soon, as does all the crew. He says he is confident of my navigational skills, yet I like to have him review all I do. Mother has been helping me, and she keeps the logbook still. The clouds have been kind and kept away all these days, so we can get observations of both sun and moon.

We raised whales twice this week but captured none.

Your cousin,

Celia

February 1, 1858

My Dearest Abigail,

The days go by and Papa gets no better. In truth, he's getting worse. He has spasms of chills, as if he were in an Arctic storm, and we cannot warm him, then a fever so high he's burning up, but we cannot cool him. Hours later, when the fever passes, he is drenched in sweat. Then it all begins again. He is so exhausted he cannot even move his head. Mother and I take turns sitting by him. I read aloud to him (Mother reads from Scripture, I read what I like), and play his favorite pieces on the melodeon.

Mother came into my cabin last night to speak to me. She said she talked with Papa about the possibility of abandoning the cruise and heading home if his condition does not improve.

"What do you think, Celia?" she asked.

It was so strange to have her seek my counsel. I told her that I would gladly be heading home and said Papa would surely recover faster there than anywhere else on earth. But Abigail, I must add that I would rather Papa was all restored to health and this cruise went on forever, than to be heading home, as I have been longing to do, because he is gravely ill.

Mother was sitting at the foot of my bunk. She stroked the quilt that was folded up there, a quilt that she had made for me some years ago. The pale blue-flowered squares, I remembered, were from a dress she often wore when I was a little girl.

"There's something else," she said. "I am concerned about Mr. Grimes. He has been overreaching his authority, and I don't like the way he runs the ship while Papa isn't about."

I waited for a minute, looking at her. She took in

her breath and smiled at me sadly. "You may have been right about him all along, Celia. I wish we had discharged him months ago."

I would have felt such triumph in her acknowledgement of that, except she looked so tired, Abigail. She's been staying up with Papa every night, and she keeps me company on deck when I take my sights and helps me work time when I can't get any observations and must rely on dead reckoning. I wonder if she ever sleeps. I put my arm around her shoulder.

"We'll manage, Mother," I said.

Love from your cousin,
Celia

February 7, 1858

My Dearest Abigail,

Now Isaac is ill as well. And Papa is even worse. He can barely eat, and he vomits when the fever strikes him, so he gets frailer every day. I saw his naked chest and arms when Mother was bathing him yesterday, and he was thin as the scarecrow in Grandmother's garden.

Without Isaac there to counter him, Mr. Grimes feels he has the freedom to do whatever he wants. He treats everyone with disdain, especially Nate. Nate has been loaded down with Isaac's duties along with his own, and I think Mr. Grimes invents new tasks just to keep him running all the time. Nate has so far managed to hold his tongue and his fists, but I wonder how long he can manage such restraint. The crew hates Mr. Grimes—I can tell that—but they are all afraid of him, except for the cooper, Mr. Beck, who does what he pleases. I sometimes see Mr. Beck conferring with Mr. Grimes, though they always move apart when I come upon them.

A whale was sighted at noon today and although the seas were so rough I could barely walk on deck, Mr. Grimes ordered the whaleboats out. He did not go himself. One boat capsized, the other two went to the rescue of the men, and thank the Lord all were saved. Papa would have rejoiced that Nate and Ephraim Millard got all the crew back alive and got the whaleboat back as well, but Mr. Grimes only said, "It's whales we're after, and if you're fools enough to lose one today, make it your business to catch at least two tomorrow."

I hope the lookout has the good sense to be unable to spot whales when the seas are too rough for any sane man to chase them.

Mother is exhausted now, caring for Isaac as well as Papa. Last night I pleaded with her to get some sleep and at last she went to bed on the sofa and let me stay up with Papa.

"Ann?" Papa asked.

"No, Papa, Mother's sleeping; it's me, Celia."

"My good girl," Papa said.

"What can I get you, Papa?" I asked him.

"Nothing. Nothing, dear."

Through the porthole I could see some small stars, struggling to be seen among the clouds. The ship rocked gently and Papa's bed creaked as it kept itself level.

"Papa, what should we do?" I asked him.

He took so long to answer I thought he hadn't heard me. Then he reached for my hand and his fingers closed over mine. "You should sail the *Jupiter* home," he said.

"But Mr. Grimes won't want—"

"Get rid of Grimes," Papa said, and it seemed to take all the energy he had. I could not bear to tell him that Isaac was ill as well. His hand slipped to the coverlet and while I sat watching him, he fell into a shallow, troubled sleep. I must have fallen asleep myself because Mother came in and helped me to my bed and I could already see the beginnings of morning through my porthole by then.

Dear Abigail. These letters will not be sent for weeks, or even months, and maybe I will be home myself before they reach you at all, but I write them still for they are one of the few comforts I have. As I write, I picture you close by, your hair falling gently over the side of your face as you tilt your head to listen to me. You have been my best listener all my life. Sometimes while I write I imagine my words can reach you in some magic way, I imagine that if you strain your ear you can hear my voice across these ruinous seas.

Dear friend, dear protector.

—Your Celia

February 8, 1858

My Dearest Abigail,

While Papa was sleeping I talked with Mother early this morning. I told her Papa said we should sail the *Jupiter* home.

"I think it may be time for us to do that," said Mother.

"Papa doesn't seem to be getting better, does he?" I asked.

Mother shook her head. "No. He isn't. I keep looking for some sign of improvement, but there is none." Mother pressed her lips together and pulled in her breath. "Celia, I fear he weakens every day."

We looked at each other. "Home?" she asked.

"Yes," I said.

Mother took my face in her hands and kissed my cheek. "When Papa is awake we'll consult with him," she said. "Then it will be decided."

"Mr. Grimes will be reluctant to abandon the cruise," I said.

"Papa is still the master of this ship," said Mother, "and Mr. Grimes will have to follow his instructions." She waited a minute, then she said, "Mr. Grimes will cause us trouble, though, I fear."

"Papa said we should get rid of him."

"There's no way we could accomplish that, Celia, and with Isaac ill, I'm afraid we have need of him."

Mother and I studied the charts together. Mother has made this return trip twice before and knows the route that Papa would take. The closest port is Valparaiso, and we decided to stop there for provisions, and to find there a doctor who can help Papa and Isaac.

When Papa was awake Mother told him about our plans. He was unable to speak, but he nodded in assent. I stayed with Papa when Mother went to inform Mr. Grimes of the decision. Toby was sitting, alert, by the foot of the bed. He's been watching over Papa since he has gotten ill.

I could hear the voices in the forecabin, Mother's calm, Mr. Grimes's rising in anger, but I could not make out what they were saying until they were standing closer to the doorway to the after-cabin.

"It is imperative I speak with him," I heard Mr. Grimes say.

"My husband is resting, Mr. Grimes," Mother said. "I will not have him be disturbed now." Her voice was stern and clear, but when she came into the cabin and closed the door behind her she was shaking so hard I put my arms around her to steady her.

Oh, Abigail. I feel as if I am ten years older than I was yesterday.

Your Celia

February 20, 1858

My Dearest Abigail,

Mr. Prater was acting strange all day, and this evening he took me aside after supper as soon as Mr. Grimes had left and whispered that he would like to speak with me. I pretended nothing had passed between us and in a loud voice I said, "Mr. Prater, I have some boxes in my cabin I need some help moving, and if you could spare me a moment this evening

I would be obliged." Mr. Prater is not the most intelligent of men, but he did catch on.

Mr. Prater was most nervous about speaking with me. He said ordinarily he would approach Mother about the matter, but she was "so busy caring for our poor Captain, dear lady," and he did not want to talk with her in Papa's presence, for he did not want to add to his worry. "And Mr. Atwood having taken sick, himself," he added, there was no one else but me.

I thought Mr. Prater would never get to what he wanted to say, but at last he did. He informed me that he'd overheard Mr. Grimes talking with the cooper. They were saying that the Captain, his wife, and daughter, and Mr. Atwood and Mr. Woodbridge were all leaving the ship at Valparaiso, and that Mr. Grimes was going to make the cooper a mate and take over the whaling venture for himself. He wondered if that was indeed the plan.

"No, Mr. Prater," I said, "that is not the plan. The plan is to sail the *Jupiter* home, with all of us aboard. Thank you for telling me what you heard. I will speak to my mother when I can, and please tell no one that you spoke with me."

He nodded. And just to make my story true I had him help me move some boxes around.

I knew Mr. Grimes would prove a traitor. Dear

Abigail, what shall we do?

I am frantic to talk with Mother, but it has not been convenient as yet, and I don't want to do anything to arouse Mr. Grimes's suspicions.

—Celia

February 21, 1858

My Dearest Abigail,

I had to wait until the middle of the night to speak to Mother. She was sitting beside Papa, tatting by a faint lamp. She was startled to see me. I motioned to her to come with me, and she laid her work down and followed me to my cabin. I told her what Mr. Prater had reported.

"I will not let Mr. Grimes take command of our ship," she said, angrily. "It's he who must be left in Valparaiso, and we must sail straight home from there without him." Then her strength deserted her. "Oh, Celia, how can we possibly manage that with Isaac now so ill himself?"

"There's Nate," I said.

"But he's so young!" Mother sighed.

"He's smart and he's able, Mother, and he's well liked by the crew."

"You say that not just because you're so fond of him?" Mother asked, and she smiled at me.

I shook my head. "You'll see, Mother, he'll earn your trust, and prove his worth."

"And the navigation—all the way back to New Bedford—it's no small task, Celia. Can you take it on?"

"With your help I can."

Mother smiled. "Papa has been so proud of you. He told me he'd trust the *Jupiter* in your hands more than any man's on the ship."

"He did?" I asked.

Mother nodded slowly. Then she hugged me close.

And here is what is most remarkable, Abigail: Mother not only solicited my opinion, but allowed herself to be guided by it! She agreed to take Nate into her confidence, and between us we devised a daring plan. I do not write it here on the remotest possibility that this letter is discovered. (I keep all my letters to you hidden in my trunk, but I can take no chances. Too much depends on it.) You shall know of it soon enough. Mother described the plan to Papa. He had no strength to speak and offer counsel, but when she asked, "Daniel, shall we risk it?" he whispered "Yes," and squeezed her hand.

We are in view now of the coastline. In a day we shall be at anchor off Valparaiso.

If all goes well this shall be the last letter I can post to you for a long time.

Pray for me.

—Celia

February 24, 1858

My Dearest Abigail,

I will not be able to post this letter, but I must write to you. So much has happened my head is swirling with it. I must set it all down. I write to steady myself, to see here in ink on paper what we have done.

We anchored yesterday morning off Valparaiso. Mr. Grimes informed Mother that she should pack up all her things and Papa's and mine, so we could disembark.

"Disembark?" asked Mother. "We have no reason to leave the ship. Find a doctor in town and bring him on board."

"Madam," said Mr. Grimes, "I'm afraid you must disembark. It is in your best interests that I suggest this course. And it is in the best interests of the Captain, and Mr. Atwood as well."

"I appreciate your consideration of my interests,

Mr. Grimes," said Mother, "but I assure you I am well able to look after them myself. And I have no intention of disembarking. It should not take long for you to secure what is necessary for the voyage home."

Mr. Grimes produced an unctuous smile. "You fail to understand me, Madam," he said. "With every concern for your welfare and that of your family, I have decided you will leave the ship and remain in this port until you secure alternate passage home. I am taking the *Jupiter* back to the New Zealand Grounds and shall be continuing this cruise."

Mother drew in her breath and looked Mr. Grimes straight in his face.

"You will do nothing of the sort, Mr. Grimes," she said. "You are not master of this ship."

"I beg your pardon, ma'am, but the Captain, your husband, is no longer in any condition to be master of this ship, as you know very well. He is no longer able to issue orders, and I am not taking orders from you."

"My father and my brother are part owners of the *Jupiter*," said Mother, "and they would want this ship to bring my husband home. If you refuse to do so, I hereby relieve you of your duties."

Mr. Grimes gave a little laugh. "Madam," he said. "You have no authority."

Mother stood facing Mr. Grimes. She gripped the edge of the table; her knuckles were white.

"Let me speak plainly, Madam," said Mr. Grimes. "As First Mate of this ship I have now, most rightly, taken over command as Captain Snow is clearly in no position to carry on with his duties. I will not abandon this cruise when it is not yet half over." He spoke as if he were addressing a maritime court. But I knew that no court would side with him, if it came to that. What he proposed was no less than mutiny.

"As a gentleman," he continued, "it is my every intention to take your welfare into account as well. But I must be clear. I will not be thwarted in my purpose, and if I do not have your cooperation I will regretfully be forced to use firmer means."

Mother let out a little gasp. She bowed her head and murmured, "Iam ego oboediens esse simulabo; tu quoque simula." She said this so Mr. Grimes would mistake it for some words of prayer. But I knew she was directing these words to me, for I was able to translate them from the Latin. What she said was "I will now pretend to cooperate; you pretend as well."

Mother released her hold of the table and sank down in the chair beside it. She put her arm around me and drew me close. "What choice do I have?" she asked.

"If you agree to leave this ship without requiring further persuasion, I will see that you are conveyed to a comfortable situation in town and shall do my best to secure you passage on a ship going directly back to New Bedford."

"And if I don't?"

"Madam, I'm afraid the consequences would be to neither of our liking."

"It seems, then, we have no choice at all."

Mr. Grimes told Mother he would give us two hours to pack our trunks and arrange for our departure. Mother protested that we would surely require considerably more time than that, but Mr. Grimes only urged us to make the greatest haste, gave a little bow, then left us alone. Mother and I hugged each other close. "Let us begin," she whispered in my ear. "May God be with us."

The progress of the conversation being no surprise to Mother and me, we pretended to be attending to our packing, but signaled to Nate that we had initiated our plan. I lay it out to you, in brief.

Nate had arranged for the cooper to win a large hand of money in a game of cards the day before, so Mr. Beck was most eager to get into port to spend it on spirits and tobacco. How relieved we were to see Mr.

Grimes and the cooper head off to shore in one of the whaleboats. Ephraim Millard, whom Nate had entrusted with the plan, was one of the crew who rowed them over, and he had no difficulty getting Mr. Beck inebriated in one of the drinking establishments in town. While Mr. Grimes was engaged at the shipping agent's office, Ephraim and the other seamen hastened to the boat and rowed back to the *Jupiter*.

Nate had the whole crew make ready for departure. We all worked, with amazing speed, to weigh anchor and set sail. Fortunately luck was with us and the wind was right. If Mr. Grimes saw us sailing out of the harbor, it was already too late for him to catch up with us.

Is this folly, Abigail?

If so, this is the first time since Papa got so ill that I have felt a weight lift off me.

—Celia

March 2, 1858

Dearest Abigail,

Papa worsens every day. He is so emaciated, Mother and I can carry him from the bed to the sofa without Mr. Prater's help. His head is still the same size, but his body is shrinking. I fear soon there will be nothing left but bones. How will he ever last until we make it home?

We planned to stop for provisions at a small island that Mother knew from a previous journey, and you can imagine how it helped my confidence as a navigator when we achieved landfall.

"You've earned the trust of all the crew," Mother told me.

I thought of that first green island where we stopped after rounding the Horn on our way out, more than a year ago. I remember how Toby ran up and down that beach, and how I wrote my name in the wet sand.

Am I that same girl?

Now we need to make it around the Horn again. We are shorthanded for whaling, but we have enough crew to sail the *Jupiter* home. Ephraim has taken on the duties of Second Mate and Nate is now First. Papa is Master in name alone, for he is not conscious much of the time. Nate told me, "I had looked forward to rising to this position, but not this suddenly, and not this way." Nate looks older now, too.

I am so afraid of the Horn I cannot let myself remember it. But there is no other way to get back home.

Dear Abigail, how could these things have happened to an ordinary girl like me?

Your cousin,
Celia

March 10, 1858

Dearest Abigail,

The sea is black. We are sucked down into deep valleys and the waves close over above us, blocking out the sky. Then we are tossed up to the peak of the next mountain, where we teeter until we plunge again. It is almost impossible to write, but I must because this may be the last letter I ever write. If I don't survive there is a chance this letter might.

I don't think we shall make it. I can see it in Nate's face, though he won't say so.

Please take care of Willie for us and let him know he had a sister who loved him dearly.

Thank you for being my dearest friend.

Adieu,
Your cousin, Celia

March 16, 1858

Dearest Abigail,

Papa died at 5:30 this morning. We made it around the Horn alive, but Papa died. It was almost that he held on until he knew that we were safe around and could make it home and then he slipped from life into death, without a word.

I am numb with grief.

There is nothing more to write.

C.

March 17, 1858

Dearest Abigail,

We have been sitting by Papa. He does not look so different dead than when he had been asleep. Mother had laid his hands upon his chest, but when the ship lurched his arms dropped down beside him. It startled us so she did not try to place them again.

I was not with Papa when he died. I was helping on deck, for there was so much damage from the storm. Mother said Papa waited until I was not in the cabin, for he would not have wanted me to watch him die, but Abby, I did not get to kiss him one last time! And after he was dead, I could touch my lips to his hair but not his skin.

When I told Isaac that Papa died, he turned his face to the wall and wept. I told him we will get him home to his Hannah. I have promised him.

—Celia

March 18, 1858

Dearest Abigail,

We had a service on deck for Papa. Ephraim read from Scripture and Nate sang a hymn. The crew presented Mother with a parchment that said they made her honorary Captain of the ship, and me an honorary Mate. They came up one by one and shook her hand and shook mine, too. Many of them were crying, and were not ashamed to do so. They have taken up a collection for a tablet in Papa's name to be placed in the Seamen's Bethel in New Bedford.

Mother would not have Papa buried at sea. We shall bring him home and bury him there. We did not have enough rum to preserve him with. His body has been coated with tar and wrapped in canvas, then placed in the box the carpenter coated inside and out with white lead. It has been placed on deck, under the spare boat. Toby scratches at it and whines. We shall have to tie him up.

How can I bear this?

—Celia

March 25, 1858

Dearest Abigail,

We are making good speed towards home. There is nothing much to write. I have been working hard as the crew, and I do not mind. I do not have to think about Papa if I am working all the time. My hands are blistered from mending sails.

Mother has been taking care of Isaac, who has not shown much improvement, but at least is getting no worse.

Nate and Ephraim have both praised me for my navigation, and I have been grateful for these clear skies so I can do my observations. It is a comfort to be on deck at twilight, with the familiar stars and planets and the moon for my guides, for, strangely, I have a sense of Papa close beside me. I can't explain it, even to you.

I always thought that when you lost someone you loved it was as if a part had been torn from inside you. But instead of something missing from my body, I feel as if there is a rock inside my belly now.

—Celia

March 27, 1858

Dearest Abigail,

Today I am fourteen. The same age that you were when I saw you last.

Mother did not forget the day. She gave me a brooch with little seed pearls that had been hers.

"Papa gave it to me, many years ago," she said, "and I want you to have it now."

When Nate learned it was my birthday he presented me with the scrimshaw whale's tooth he's been carving. He has been working on this piece for months and I am sure it was intended for his family at home. It is a picture of the *Jupiter* in full sail, with flags flying and a whale diving under the bow. There is a circle of leaves all around and a rose carved on the other side.

"I will inscribe your name on it, when I have the time," he said. "Celia Elizabeth Snow, Mate."

I looked up at him, but instead of giving him my

thanks, I burst into tears instead.

There is only one thing that could make me happy on this birthday. And it is the one thing that I can't have.

Your cousin,
Celia

April 4, 1858

Dearest Abigail,

I thought that nothing could make me smile again, but something has happened that did. We've met up with the Winslows! They had made it around the Horn barely three weeks ahead of us and have been cruising the Atlantic since.

How wonderful it was to hug Robin and Content close to me, to have them really alive. How wonderful it was to have Mary's arms around me, her kisses on my face. How wonderful it was to have Captain Winslow give me a great bear hug of his.

And yet, how terrible to hear him ask, "But where is Daniel?" and see Mary suddenly take notice of Mother's black dress and cry out, "No!" They all wept over our great loss.

"Your Papa would be proud of you," Captain

Winslow told me after they had heard the tale of all our hardships and how we had outwitted Mr. Grimes.

As for the rumor of their tragedy. The *Ranger* that ran aground on a reef and was wrecked was a bark, not a ship, and it was out of New London, not Edgartown. Mrs. Doane got much of it wrong, for all but two members of the crew were saved and the Captain never had wife or children aboard.

The Winslows have offered to give up their cruise and take us directly to New Bedford, but Mother insists we are managing well.

"Celia and I are bringing this ship home together," she said, and she took my hand. "We are doing this for Daniel. He would want it so."

Captain Winslow asked if as a favor she would take on two of his crew who would like a speedy return to New Bedford, and she did agree. I suspect he paid them off to go because he knew that we are short of crew and wanted us to get home as quickly as we can. He is so generous a man, he has given us a wealth of provisions, knowing we have been running short since we were not able to stock up in Valparaiso.

We gammed with the Winslows for two days running, and I hated to leave them again.

Captain Winslow told me to remember that they are "indestructible" and that we will certainly see them once again. Somehow I feel that this is true.

Your cousin,
Celia

April 18, 1858

My Dearest Abigail,

The winds have been good to us and we have been making excellent time.

It is warm enough to write in my favorite perch, the waistboat. I sit so I am facing out at sea, for I do not want to have the spare boat in view and see the edge of Papa's box. I do not like to think of his body in there, the canvas tight around him, all coated with tar, even over his dear face.

Yesterday evening I asked Mother where we were going to bury Papa.

She seemed surprised. "Why, in the cemetery," she said, "in the family plot. If only Sallie were laid to rest there, too!"

"Will he be buried beside Demaris?" I asked.

"Demaris? What do you know of her?"

"I know that she was Papa's first wife. She died while he was away on a cruise, soon after they were first married. Her stone is there in the cemetery."

"That's all true, Celia. Demaris—we called her 'Merry'—died when she was so young."

"You knew her, then?"

"Certainly I knew her. Papa's family lived in the house across the road from ours. She moved there when she was married. Not four months after the wedding Papa left on a whaling cruise—he was a first mate then and could not take a bride along—and she was left behind, with her husband's parents. I was just a young girl then, and she was so kind to me. She sewed dresses for my dolls and taught me how to ice skate on Great Pond. She was lonely, I knew, away from her own family."

"You did not hate her, then?"

"Hate her? Why should you say that? No, I loved her! Everyone who knew her did. When she got ill I prayed for her every day, and when she died—Oh, Celia, I was devastated."

"Weren't you in love with Papa then?"

"In love with Papa then!" Mother gave a little laugh. "Oh, Celia, I was just a girl then; I thought of him as an old man. He was an old man to me. Of course I felt very sad for him when he came home to find his bride had been buried for many months. He left soon after that for another cruise, and I did not see him again till he came home after a number of years at sea."

"And you fell in love with him then?"

"No. I had fallen in love with a young man whom my parents did not approve of. They thought him unsteady, and although I suspected they were right, I loved him nonetheless."

"And what became of him?"

"He shipped out on a whaler and promised he would make his fortune and come back to marry me. I got but one letter from him (I must have written him a hundred) and then the report that he had deserted the ship in California. Nothing more."

"And then you fell in love with Papa?"

"I will tell you, Celia. It was different with Papa. He was twelve years older than me, and I never would have considered marrying him. It was another five years before he was back in Eastham again. By then I was older, and I had given up on my first love. I had been hurt and bitter and then, resigned. Both your uncles had married, as well as your aunt, my younger sister, and I was the only one left at home. Your grandmother and

I bickered all the time. I feared I'd be a spinster, cooped up there forever, so when Papa asked me to marry him, I agreed."

Mother loosened her lace collar and rubbed her neck. I was afraid she was done talking to me even though the tale did not seem over. She closed her eyes for a moment, and then she took in her breath and looked at me.

"I did not love Papa then, but I respected him, and knew him to be a gentle man. Loving him came after. Some women marry for love and after a number of years they are disenchanted. With me, Celia, it was just the opposite. The more I knew your father, the more I came to love him. And you have proof of that, for much as I hate to be at sea, whenever I could I chose to be with him. I would rather be with him, even in the roughest ocean, than apart from him in the grandest house in town."

I sat there for a moment. I thought about how I'd had things all wrong.

"I thought you disliked Nate because he reminded you of Merry," I said. "I had thought she was your rival."

"Oh, Celia!" Mother exclaimed. "It was for her sake that I pleaded with Papa to take him on as third mate. Papa thought Nate was too young and inexperienced, but I persuaded Papa to give him a chance. If ever I seemed hard on him it was only because I wanted so much for him to succeed."

So I had been wrong about that, too, Abigail.

All these months together on this ship and Mother and I had never talked about these things before. It seems as if it is so much easier for her to tell me things now. Maybe it is because now I really want to listen.

Your loving cousin,
Celia

April 30, 1858

Dearest Abigail,

There has not been much to write about these past days. The good news is that Isaac has been feeling somewhat better. Nate and Mr. Prater carried him up on deck. He tilted his face up to the sun. "I thought I would never see it again," he said.

The men have been painting the ship (though I feel their hearts are not in it). Mother says that Papa always took great pride in having the *Jupiter* look her best when they returned home, and she would not have it shabby now.

Every now and then I have a whiff of home. I feel a little stirring of anticipation, but it fades as soon as it is kindled. You have no inkling that we are so soon returning, and are innocent still of our grief. My poor, dear Willie! How different this homecoming shall be from what I had been savoring in my imagination all those long months!

We are bringing Papa's body back, but Papa is left somewhere far behind us. Papa, the person that he was, is as good as buried in the sea.

—Celia

May 2, 1858

My Dearest Abigail,

Nate and I were sitting at the end of dinner today, Mother had taken tea to Isaac, and Mr. Prater was carrying out the dishes, muttering as he does, this time about the lack of wind. It made me think of that day so long ago at the beginning of the trip when he had predicted bad luck because we set sail on a Friday. I asked Nate if he thought we should have listened to Mr. Prater then.

"No, Celia," said Nate. "That was just foolish superstition."

"That's what Papa said, and yet Mr. Prater was proved right."

"No, he wasn't right."

"But look what's happened—"

"Things always happen, Celia. That's what whaling cruises are like. There are always dangers and illnesses. No ship comes home without its losses along with its oil, and sometimes there's no oil, and sometimes the ship never makes it home."

"Then why choose such a life?" I asked.

Nate shrugged. "I wonder, sometimes, and yet I ask myself if there is any life where things are safe for sure, and even on dry land, Celia, there isn't one. And so you might as well choose a life you want."

I thought about that. Isaac said he would be a farmer if he could. But Papa—well, I must admit that I can't imagine Papa choosing anything other than to be master of a whaleship.

Your most affectionate cousin,
Celia

May 5, 1858

Dearest Abigail,

We are so close to home but have made little head-way these past few days, the wind so unfairly favoring those ships (three have passed us just today) who are outward bound.

Mother and Mr. Prater have been in a frenzy of cleaning and packing. I am glad I have the navigation to attend to. I told Mother I did not think it mattered if all the spoons were polished well.

"That's true, of course," she said, and she laughed, "but I suppose I find my comfort in getting right the things I can, for then I worry less about the things I can't."

Isaac tried to take a few steps yesterday, but the sea refused to cooperate and with the first roll of the ship he plopped right down and pulled Nate with him.

"We'll have you dancing yet!" said Nate.

Toby won't let me out of his sight. I am constantly tripping over him while I try to organize my trunks and boxes. I've packed away my books and most of my clothes, including the green silk dress that I had once looked forward to wearing when we arrived back in New Bedford. I remember how I would take it out and hold it up against me and twirl around, dreaming of dancing along the cobbled streets. How everything changes. Now I will be in the mourning dress that Mother made for me. And it hardly matters to me what I wear.

Your loving cousin,
Celia

May 8, 1858

Dearest Abigail,

Last night was so warm, Mother and I stayed up late, sitting on deck. The sea was calm enough to be a mirror for the sky, and the *Jupiter* was still as a building on land.

Mother said she had something she had been wanting to tell me. She said I had been right about Nate: he had proved to be worthy of our trust. She wanted me to know that she was grateful that I stood up for him.

"You are too young to have a sweetheart," she told me, "but when you are old enough to think of such things, I would feel glad if you chose as fine a man as he, and I'm sure that Papa would, too."

Mother is right, I am too young, but maybe by the time I'm old enough Nate will be single still. Someday he'll be Captain for sure. And I think I would not mind, myself, being a captain's wife.

Your cousin,
Celia

May 14, 1858

My Dearest Abigail,

Land is in sight. Before tomorrow night we shall reach New Bedford, and if the wind holds we'll go right up the Acushnet River into the harbor.

This is the last letter I shall write to you on the *Jupiter*. I wonder how many of the ones I wrote ever made it safely to you, and how many of them are lost forever or on ships somewhere, seeking their way home.

Home: the place I have been longing to be for so many months. Yet "home" will always mean the *Jupiter*, too—my little cabin, with the narrow bunk against the wall, my seat at the table under the skylight, my perch in the waistboat.

I stand on the deck and look out at the sea, memorizing the wind against my face, the rail beneath my hands, memorizing who I am now.

Papa is dead but still I feel him right here inside me. I grieve for him, but it is a grief I can carry.

"The only thing you can rely on is yourself," Papa told me, "and the people you love."

I think he must have known that Mother and I would find each other in the end.

Your most loving cousin,
Celia